The Burning Bush

Also by Robert Drake
Fiction
AMAZING GRACE
THE SINGLE HEART
Criticism
FLANNERY O'CONNOR (Contemporary Writers in Christian
   Perspective Series)
(Edited) *THE WRITER AND HIS TRADITION* (Proceedings of
   the 1969 Southern Literary Festival)

ST. PHILIPS COLLEGE LIBRARY

The Burning Bush
and
Other Stories

by
Robert Drake

AURORA PUBLISHERS, INC.
NASHVILLE / LONDON

"The Burning Bush." Copyright © 1972 Christian Century Foundation. Reprinted by permission from the November 29, 1972 issue of *The Christian Century*.

"Christmas Sorrows, Christmas Joys." Copyright © 1972 Christian Century Foundation. Reprinted by permission from the December 20, 1972 issue of *The Christian Century*.

Selections from "Tree at My Window" and "After Apple Picking" from *The Poetry of Robert Frost* edited by Edward Connery Lathem. Copyright 1928, 1930, 1939, © 1969 by Holt, Rinehart and Winston, Inc. Copyright © 1956, 1958 by Robert Frost. Copyright © 1967 by Lesley Frost Ballentine. Reprinted by permission of Holt, Rinehart and Winston, Inc.

Lines from "Sailing to Byzantium" reprinted with permission of Macmillan Publishing Co., Inc. from *Collected Poems* by William Butler Yeats. Copyright 1928 by Macmillan Publishing Co., Inc. Renewed 1956 by Georgia Yeats.

COPYRIGHT © 1975 BY
AURORA PUBLISHERS INCORPORATED
NASHVILLE, TENNESSEE 37203
LIBRARY OF CONGRESS CATALOG CARD NUMBER: 73-93410
STANDARD BOOK NUMBER: 87695-171-X
MANUFACTURED IN THE UNITED STATES OF AMERICA

*This book is dedicated to
the memory of
Auntee
who was
Blanche Wood Hellen
and
Aunt Weedy
who was
Eloise Pierson Drake*

Acknowledgments

"The Burning Bush" and "Christmas Sorrows, Christmas Joys" appeared originally in *The Christian Century*.
"The Dream House" appeared originally in *The Georgia Review*.
"A Peacock on a Sparrow's Back" appeared originally in *Modern Age*.
"Wake Up So I Can Tell You Who's Dead" appeared originally in *The South Carolina Review*.

    I am grateful to the editors of these periodicals for permission to include these stories in this volume. It is also a pleasure to record here my indebtedness to the Department of English at the University of Tennessee, Knoxville, and its Hodges Better English Fund for benefits by no means forgot.

—R.D.

Contents

The Burning Bush	1
Mild Turbulence	7
The Tent Show	13
You're Not Going to Die Till Your Time Comes	19
The Death in the Dream	25
Under the Bluff	33
Where Did the Music Go?	41
A Perfect Lady	47
The Sweetest One of All	53
Wake Up So I Can Tell You Who's Dead	57
I Didn't Go On With My Music	67
The Dream House	73
A Very Powerful Woman	81
A Killing Frost	89
This Tremendous Lover	97
What Would You Do In Real Life?	105
A Peacock on a Sparrow's Back	113
O, What a One To Be Dead With!	119
Honk if You Love Jesus	125
Show the Gentleman What You Have	131
What Papa Said	139
I've Been Dying All My Life; How About You?	145
What Do You Want to Have Written on Your Tombstone?	151
Troubled Sleep	157
Christmas Sorrows, Christmas Joys	161

An aged man is but a paltry thing,
A tattered coat upon a stick, unless
Soul clap its hands and sing, and louder sing
For every tatter in its mortal dress. . . .
—William Butler Yeats, "Sailing to Byzantium"

And the angel of the Lord appeared unto him in a flame of fire out of the midst of a bush: and he looked, and, behold, the bush burned with fire, and the bush was not consumed.
—Exodus 3:2

And he said unto me, Son of man, can these bones live? And I answered, O Lord God, thou knowest.
—Ezekiel 37:3

The Burning Bush

My mother always called it a japonica, but most people I knew called it a burning bush. There was one right at our front doorstep, and every spring it was among the first shrubs to bloom, along with the forsythia and bridal wreath. Its blossoms were small red flowers—really almost a salmon pink. And I always wondered why anyone had called it by the more familiar name: it didn't look like it was really afire, and it didn't in the least remind you of the bush God had spoken to Moses out of. But somehow the name had stuck, for a good many generations, it would seem; and I imagine many people would have thought the botanical name of japonica too highfalutin and grand.

There was certainly nothing grand about the burning bush: they grew everywhere, in formally tended gardens, in disarray in some vacant lot, sometimes even almost wild in front of a Negro cabin. And you could drive along the road early in March and see the first spring sunshine tangling itself in the branches and kindling both them and the blooms until they almost seemed ready to burst into cold fire, silver flame. Was there a parable in it all—that the Creation, no matter how seemingly insignificant in some of its parts, no matter how abused and demeaned by man, was still the Lord's and that it lay forever in His hand, good and bad, ugly and beautiful?

I used to wonder about such matters when I was growing up—the seeming determination on the part of many people to ennoble the everyday world around them, and see in it a splendor which I felt signally lacking. Splendor, glory, beauty, I then thought, were reserved for the movies, Technicolor, Hollywood or else the world of literature, with swashbuckling heroes, perfidious villains, glamorous fair-haired heroines, and dark seductive temptresses. Or else they lay far off in place and time, with Queen Elizabeth I, Lord Nelson, and General Lee—always with old unhappy far-off things, in faery lands forlorn. Any time but

THE BURNING BUSH

now; any place but here: that was where romance and beauty dwelt. Certainly, they were not present in the japonica, the burning bush, no matter by what name it was called. In fact, wasn't it but a perversion of romance, in another direction, to call the plant by its botanical name instead of the more familiar colloquial one? It was still nothing but an old gray bush that, once a year, for only a few days, produced some small off-red blooms.

By the time I had arrived at that view of things—both personal and public—I had been gone from the South and my childhood for a good many years: I was twenty-five and working at a job I didn't particularly like in Chicago. But at least I had proved I could get away from home, that I was grown up, and that I had gotten outside the South, which, I had come to think, had for far too long had its head in the sand—ostrich-like—where modern times and progress were concerned. And no, I didn't have a hang-up about racial guilt on the part of the white Southerner; I certainly didn't have Negroes on the brain either. And I was sure I had lost whatever romantic illusions I had ever cherished about Southern history—perhaps any history. After all, hadn't it been recorded that General Lee's last words were not something memorable and heartbreaking about the Lost Cause but a bald, blunt request for the bedpan?

Southerners, I had come to think, were not merely wrapped up in the Southern past and gimcrack romance; they were just too involved in context, period. It didn't seem to matter to them what you were so much as who you were, where you were from, and who your folks had been before you. And many of them were certainly making a lifework out of "what Papa said" and "back when things were normal," which I thought nothing but history-worship, to escape the present. Or else they discoursed on personal beauty, as if there were some sort of inherent virtue in the looks you were either born with or without. (How many times had I heard: "She's a good old soul but the ugliest white woman you ever saw in your life" or else "I saw him down town the other day, and I couldn't get over how he had failed—not a tooth in his head"?) My God, the way you looked didn't have

The Burning Bush

anything to do with the way you *were;* and I had about reached the stage where I wasn't overly long on lilies of the field anyhow. I myself had had to take considerable thought for the morrow; nobody had ever paid me just to sit around and look pretty. And I had never been able to make a career out of who my father had been or what he had said or done. I was up and doing and earning my living, and I wasn't going to drown in a context to please anybody.

So I rocked along for a good many years, rising in my job's ranks and making more and more money. And God knows I was certainly up and doing enough to please Henry W. Grady or Henry W. Longfellow or anybody else. But somehow a vague disquiet had crept into my bloodstream, and I noticed that this unrest always seemed to be sharper and more apparent after I had been home for my yearly visit. I wasn't sure why, either. They were all of them—what family and friends were left—the same as ever: they still wanted to know the who-shot-John and who was Peter's wife's mother and where they were from about everybody they met. And the family as a unit was still as powerful—and as demanding—as ever. Once one of the uncles expressed surprise, almost shock, when a lady of our acquaintance remarked of an old friend who had just died: "I never had a better friend in my life than she was." My uncle was incredulous: "And you mean she wasn't even *kin* to her?" He couldn't imagine any kind of relationship that could transcend the blood tie. And of course I soon realized that, as far as my family and others there were concerned, there was nothing one could do to justify his existence more effectually than simply to reproduce his kind, with or without benefit of clergy. Quite literally, it seemed to cover a multitude of sins; and of course it insured the continuity if not the perpetuity of the family, though I thought they might have been more particular about some of the terms of the insurance policy. But not so. They were all of them, I thought, drowning in what one of my less reverent friends called young-love, mother-love, and baby-love. Alas for the childless bachelor in such a setting; he was time's eunuch indeed. He could of course

THE BURNING BUSH

be tolerated, after all, he was *from* there, in the beginning. But he was viewed with alarm too; why had he left, and wasn't he getting above his raising anyhow, with his big-city attitudes and ways?

I found it, year after year, partially infuriating but, as I said, also disquieting. Were their values, however much I might dislike them, more solidly based than my own? Had I paid too big a price for my mess of pottage? True, I was up and doing, but doing what? The world I moved in didn't seem to care, yet I knew somehow it did matter and that my family would care. The world I lived in took you for what you were, so they said; and they couldn't care less where you were *from. Context* was a vain and idle word to them, yet I knew somehow it was more than that, even if I couldn't precisely buy it as packaged and delivered at home.

Perhaps I would never have honestly confronted the dilemma—or at least not for some time to come—had I not had to go home recently to bury one of the last of the uncles. My Chicago friends had accused me of playing the "Down Home" game with them when I regaled them with tales of home and family life in the Deep South, yet I knew that I had not altogether uprooted myself from there and perhaps never could. I could, at any rate, view it with a more dispassionate gaze for having been away so long. (I was now thirty-five: ten years on the shores of Lake Michigan.) And I was used to going home to bury the old folks; it had become almost a ritual, formalized and codified in all its general routines. Before long, I thought, they would all be gone from that generation. Something else would have to call me home then. Would it be duty, curiosity, or what?

It was early spring when my uncle died, and he was buried in the family plot on a raw gusty day—the kind that makes you wonder whether the whole vernal thing hasn't been premature and there may be blizzards yet to come. But as we turned into the cemetery drive, I saw that a burning bush in a lot some distance from ours had burst into full bloom and was tossing to and fro as if to defy the cold snap—sparkling in the feeble sunshine,

The Burning Bush

perhaps brave, surely jolly. And it gripped the earth with a fierce tenacity. As we followed my uncle's coffin up the path, one of the widowed aunts who was leaning on my arm whispered, "See that burning bush? Old Mrs. Perkins—not any kin to us except by marriage—planted it there over fifty years ago. I remember it as a young girl. And it's still in business at the same place after all these years. And that's more than you can say for lots of folks. And every time I've come here for a funeral I sort of like to nod to it to let it know I've still got my eye on it, and it's never disappointed me yet. And somehow I feel like it's got its eye on me too—like God and Moses that time. It's kind of silly, I guess; but many of the things that help to keep us going are, I suppose."

That's been several months ago now, but I haven't been able to get that picture of the burning bush out of my mind. Did it speak to me too that day, commanding me to forsake the land of the Pharaohs for the quiet green fields, the slow, still waters of home? God help me; I don't know. Did it really have any message for me other than the enigmatic "I am that I am"? Again, I'm not sure. Could there be an implicit judgment on me in such a fancied proclamation? I had always thought that was the Old Testament in a nutshell—the continual confrontation of the erring Jews by the great I AM and His imperative "Who do you think you are anyhow?" Troubling reflections indeed. I certainly couldn't discuss them with anybody here in the office. But the bush continues to burn in my mind, without being consumed; and the other day I even caught myself looking out of the office window at the scurrying hordes below on the street and saying somewhat wistfully, under my breath, "Can these bones live?"

Mild Turbulence

We are sitting on the front porch one hot summer night, talking to some cousins we see every day yet never have time really to *visit* with. And all is dark except for the light which spills out from our tall living room windows and the street light directly across from us on the corner, where we children sometimes play when there is nothing going on at home. My mother and one of the cousins sit in the swing, which creaks slowly but regularly as they idly push it back and forth. They don't seem to be planning to get anywhere; it's just something they do, to keep the conversation and the visit going. My father sits in the big high-back rocker that belonged to his father, the only grandparent I ever knew, the one we all called "Pa." His big cigar alternately glows and fades as he puffs on it, as if underlining or even punctuating his conversation. And he doesn't rock; he smokes: that's his rhythm as distinguished from the ladies' rocking. The only other sounds, over the creak of the swing and the rise and fall of the conversation, are the July flies screeching in unison from our trees; the only other light, the lightning bugs winking fitfully in the dark.

I sit there quietly in the shadows, for I am a child and children should be seen and not heard. How old? I don't know exactly, and perhaps it doesn't really matter. What one never forgets, though, in this particular world is that between the life of a child and the arena of the adults, there is a great gulf fixed. And rarely is it ever crossed from the child's side. But a child can listen, and that's what I do now, as the voices talk on into the darkness, on into the night—now aimless, now pointed, but never silent. The real silence is in me, where I take the voices, unconsciously, unwittingly recovered, to some inner solitude, where I can examine them at leisure, not only as they speak in actuality but as, later on, they re-echo in my head. And this solitude is like some holy place, some inner shrine where none can enter except by my

THE BURNING BUSH

leave; and I see myself there as hugging myself in delight at the inviolability of my citadel and the treasures of memory held safe there. Perhaps what the voices say is not so important as that they are then mine, to ponder and make of what I will—something I rarely am allowed to do in the world of daylight, the world of the adults. And it is this distant sanctuary I retreat into now, out of the night, out of the talk, yet taking as much of it with me as I need or require.

And my need is for dreams—and not just the childhood ones of make-believe, either. Nor are they what later the world will call the wish-fulfillment fantasies of a teen-ager. My dreams are what I make of what I hear; I am their lord and master; they are the me answerable only to myself, the joy no one can ever take from me. Surely they not only define but extend my own identity; in them only do I truly practice myself, then know myself. The rest seems but time-serving, world-serving—the world, I'm sure, of the adults.

But what do the voices I hear on the front porch say? Nothing, yet everything. They all have to do with the right here, the immediate now, with the past very much alive in the present, with "'what Papa said" and "who so-and-so was before she married," and with blood will tell and murder will out. Here the sins of the fathers are indeed visited upon the children, and that right soon. One doesn't even have to wait for the third and fourth generations. Death flits in and out of the talk, of course, a sinister presence yet one altogether natural and acceptable. Whether one fears it or hates it or has already made some sort of working arrangement—a private truce—with it, doesn't seem to matter. It's there, written into the contract, part of the deal. And no one complains about it.

No more than he complains of the passage of time, really. The past, for these speakers, is still alive and well, living on into the present, on into them. It's but another part of the continuum which also includes present and future, and all are part of some great eternal whole. Even the child which I am can sense that— the drama of eternity, which is both now and also yesterday and

Mild Turbulence

tomorrow. The characters which populate this stage are the living and the dead, sometimes even generations yet to come. It's all the same to these speakers, all the same to me. To them—and to me—time and mortality are not an affront or an accident but the skin in which we are encased. No time, no death, no them, no me: that's what it all adds up to.

The most obvious and immediate setting for the drama realized in the voices which becomes also the drama of my dreams is of course the family—the stage where all points of this eternity meet, perhaps a secular communion of saints in which neither time nor place finally avails, though neither must be discounted as an actuality, the stuff of which daily life is made. But the same conflicts, the old collisions, the same wild loves, the same fierce hates persist time after time, year after year, where everything changes, yet nothing changes. And I listen greedily for real tales of flesh-and-blood characters. That they have actually lived, that they are many of them kin to me perhaps gives them and their actions an extra hold over me. But, again, it's not what they are already that I take final hold of; it's what they become in that secret place in my mind, where they act predictably and according to rule and meaning. What real life so seldom provides. There, in the "real" world, the patterns must be discerned, often very fugitive and fleeting ones indeed. It is otherwise, though, in my private world.

Now the voices swell louder, as my father tells some mildly risqué anecdote. One of his favorites is about the woman riding bareback up to the porch of a country store over in Arkansas and asking the loafers there if she is headed the right way to a little town named Stretchit. There are giggles and cluckings which of course fool no one; they're all delighted with the tale, even for the twentieth time. And my father's big cigar glows with triumph as he approaches, then takes the hurdle of the punch line, like the skillful and practiced jumper he is.

Then the voices dwindle down into quietness as someone remembers that a relative is ill, perhaps not expected to recover; and we may be regaled with all the grotesqueries of the sickroom

THE BURNING BUSH

or even the funeral parlor. This naturally leads to other deaths, other sadnesses, which may, in turn, come full circle round into who was whose mother-in-law on the other side of the house and who Great-Grandmother was before she married and began those endless Biblical "begats." Birth, death, love, hate: it matters not, finally. They're all real. And they all go into my place of dreams.

Those dreams of childhood, of course, are not dead now but very much alive and very independent. And they do not necessarily come when you do call for them, either. I've learned that long since, I hope. One commands them, in the sense that he tries to shape them into the meaningful patterns he misses in the wide world outside, the world of daylight, the old world of the adults. Yet again, the dreams can be stronger than we are; and they lay hold of us—or can do so—to delight but also to disturb. Perhaps they even drive us to try to make them public; hence we *create,* whether in conversation or writing or some other art form. In the act of bringing them forth, we learn more their nature and perhaps their significance for us, their hold on us. Not the nightmare of the melodramatic whirlwind, whether God speaks out of it or no, but the "mild turbulence" of a routine jet flight: that's what they're more apt to give us, in the plain "human sleep" of Frost's apple-picking poem, which is not untroubled by plain human dreams, for the very reason that a man *is* a man and not a woodchuck.

It's this mild turbulence which crept into my blood from those hot summer nights so long ago, to trouble my dreams, unsettle my waking hours. Yet how can it be otherwise, if one is to live, if one is to feel? The dream and the actuality can never be precisely one; we labor all our lives sometimes under that delusion. Yet who is to say us nay in the attempt? Is not a vulgar, even impossible, dream better than no dream at all? Can not a case be made for even the gorgeousness of the Silver Screen in the Golden Days of Hollywood? Take away our dreams and we die: that seems certain, sad as they may seem, lonely as they appear.

My own dreams first gave me a private world of my own.

Mild Turbulence

Later, I came to see that they need not constitute merely an escape from whatever one found unpleasant in his own life. Indeed, they seemed essential in defining that very round of day-to-day living decreed by the daylight world where one earns his bread. Today, these many years later, I still hear those voices speaking in the darkness on the front porch, then passing on into the twilight world of dreams where they still abide, murmuring quietly, mildly turbulent but beyond loss, beyond sadness now, even at times, like Whitman's "dumb, beautiful ministers," heralds of some wonder, messengers of great joy.

The Tent Show

The tent show that came to town every fall (fall for the tent show and spring for the carnival—all to get the money out of the Negroes, from their cotton or strawberry picking, as the case might be, Mamma said) was not really named the tent show. It was actually called Winstead's Comedians; but that didn't seem really right either since they put on plays that were not altogether funny, as well as the broad, slapstick farces that most people liked. I know one year they put on *The Trail of the Lonesome Pine,* which required two special trucks, they said, just to haul its scenery in; and I wouldn't have considered that a funny play, though of course I might have been remembering the movie version, seen some years before, in which a little boy was blown up in a steam shovel—perhaps blown up *by* it, for all I could recollect. But, nevertheless, it had been a horrible moment, safe though I was, in my nurse Louella's arms in the colored gallery of the Dixie Theater.

I suppose now Mr. Winstead, who ran his own troupe with what I imagine was a very firm paternal hand, liked the name "comedians": it sounded jolly but still gave all the leeway he needed, for laughter or for tears. Perhaps he even fancied its "classical" sound. Still, to all of us, it was simply the tent show, just as the carnival was still the carnival and not "Major Vinton's Broadway Show of Shows" or something like that. And it *was* under a tent, which was one of the best parts of all—like going to a circus or something else that gained something from the very fact that it was only temporarily housed. Gaiety, joy, whatever had to soar high in the shadow of such transience. Because every Sunday they moved on to another small town, in time for another grand opening on Monday night, usually with a comedy that Mr. Winstead always described to the audience as "clean and wholesome as you'd ever want to see." At the time I couldn't imagine a play that was anything else: what would an *unclean*

THE BURNING BUSH

play be anyhow? But when I asked Mamma, she just said it meant the play would be entertaining and uplifting instead of glum and depressing. But I don't know that that satisfied me either.

The tent show always performed on the vacant lot right across from the Baptist Church, and I suppose it was pointed out by the Baptist preacher as a snare and a delusion for the unwary. But I heard Daddy tell Mamma once that every Wednesday night, when the tent show was in town for its annual week, Mr. Winstead sent the Baptist preacher, Brother Hornsby, a check for ten dollars—which I suppose was to help cover his loss in gate receipts at prayer meeting. Anyhow, Daddy said he thought it was a fine gesture. I don't remember what Mamma said. Probably just pursed her lips and raised her eyebrows: she wasn't long on gestures, though she was a firm believer in putting your money where your mouth was. I realize all this about them now, though of course I couldn't have told you any of it in so many words at the time. And I never heard of Brother Hornsby returning the check either.

Anyhow, the Monday night play was usually the clean, wholesome comedy, along the lines of "clean, corn-fed or hometown boy saves pretty girl from clutches of city-slicker villain," not by violence so much as by ridicule and making her see the error of her ways. Then, as the week went along, the plays would progress through other variations on this theme (they were definitely geared for rural and small-town audiences), through a glorious "red-headed Toby show," with one of that immortal band of carrot-topped jokesters pulling out all the stops and doing his utmost to discomfit the proud, the haughty, and the phony, up until Saturday night (the Toby show was usually on Friday, as a treat for all the school children who might not have been allowed to go on a school night) when the "spectacular" took place—whatever was the grandest trick in the tent show's bag and required the most scenery and the most characters. If it wasn't *The Trail of the Lonesome Pine,* it would be something else like *The Shepherd of the Hills* or something like that. And

The Tent Show

then, having brought *living* glory (not even the picture show could compete with that) into town for a week, they would depart, leaving life all the drearier for a few days. But youth springs back, you know; and a few days later we would be full of a new song, a new radio program, a new picture show, something. We didn't lie down and die when the tent show left, though there was a terrible temptation to at times.

Of course, you could see through the glamor, as you got older: Mrs. Winstead, who usually played the more innocent and helpless heroines, lathered inch-deep with make-up and corseted within an inch of her life and selling tickets out front; the spotty orchestra, with the seedy looking trombone player, the jaded drummer staring idly into space, not even listening to what they were playing, and the gray-haired harridan jumping up and down on the piano stool in time to the music as though she were controlled by a spring, never batting an eye of either pleasure or pain. There was the come-on of the candy sale, before the play began, where you bought a nickel box of taffy and hoped there would be a coupon for a prize inside. (O, those beautiful teddy bears! Those fabulous Oriental rugs so opulently displayed before the curtain!) But when you did get a prize, it turned out to be something you hadn't even seen from the audience: a made-in-Japan mechanical pencil or compact or something. Nothing really grand at all, yet still a prize and you couldn't ignore that. After the play there would be another extra added attraction, for which you paid again: the concert, where the tired old band would do specialty numbers and the vocalist would croon the latest songs from The Hit Parade. But Mamma and Daddy would usually insist on going home at that point: they thought I'd had enough too, I know.

But one of the greatest of moments came during one of the intermissions when Mr. Winstead, who was also on the bill as a magician, would put on one of his magic acts, though I never did get to see him tie the girl up, lock her in the trunk, and then at the count of "three," produce her from behind a screen across the stage. All my friends, I think, must have seen it; and they

15

THE BURNING BUSH

talked about little else for several days. But I had to sit that one out and remember mainly other feats of Mr. Winstead's where "the hand was quicker than the eye," as he called it. And somehow I wished he wouldn't say that: it seemed somehow to be low-rating what he was doing, undermining his profession, I suppose. Sure, you knew there wasn't any real *magic* involved; yet why not pretend there was? It was as much fun as Santa Claus, even when you'd found out about him. Anyhow, it was great to see Mr. Winstead produce live pigeons from his top hat (yes, he really wore full evening dress, which we all thought very grand), and pull countless pastel scarves from the sleeves of some pretty actress' long dress.

And once there was even a levitation number: one of the prettier girls in the company got put into a trance and then lifted up about five feet high in the air, with Mr. Winstead running a big hoop back and forth over her, to show there were no concealed wires or strings. That part—the putting the girl in a trance—had a morbid fascination for me, like letting them put you to sleep in a hospital—something strange and unnatural, I thought. And hypnotizing the girl in the furniture store window to advertise Beauty Rest mattresses affected me the same way too. There was something sinister about it, I thought. Who wanted to be put to sleep by somebody else, put into their power, to do goodness knows what with? It made me weak in the knees and in the stomach, just to think about it. (Maybe it was too much like the spells of fairy tales worked by wicked witches and heartless enchanters.)

As the years went by, I could see that a lot of the glamor of the Winstead troupe was a tawdry thing, as I said before. I eventually learned to dislike their false, elocution-type voices, their overly dramatic gestures, their very plays themselves. They were all black and white, with no middle ground in them: straight melodrama, I realized. And it was all neither true to art nor true to life. A lot of my contemporaries agreed, too. If I could have seen into the future, I might have been made still sadder: the days of Winstead's Comedians were indeed numbered, as more

The Tent Show

and more people deserted them for the movies and then later television, which must have really signed the troupe's death warrant. No living band of the sort likely to come through our town could compete with such attractions as that. They had had a very real place in the minds and affections of all the folks at home, but that place would finally be preempted by other forms of entertainment. And I don't know that you could have called the audience fickle either; they were moving with the times, and Winstead's Comedians had had its day. At any rate, that's what they would have said.

I couldn't know that when I was growing up of course, when the annual week that Winstead's Comedians spent with us seemed one of the most magical that ever was. The plays always ended right, the pretty and good folks got the rewards, and the ugly or bad ones got their just deserts. It was a perfect economy, I thought. Yet, all along, perhaps there were disquieting signs that, not even in this Arcadia, was all as it might be. I know the year they came, when I was about six, there was the most beautiful teddy bear you ever saw displayed with the prizes every night during the candy sale. He was about three feet tall (almost as tall as I was!) and cinnamon in color, dressed in blue overalls. And I wanted him so badly I could practically taste him. Night after night—well, the nights I was allowed to go, either with my parents or Louella, and I would fall asleep in somebody's lap before the play was over, like as not—I would buy as many boxes of nickel taffy as Daddy or Mamma would let me. But no prize or else just a coloring book, when I took the coupon up to the resplendently dressed lady who presided on the stage. Finally, on Saturday night, after I had once again had no luck, Daddy announced that we would leave right after the candy show and not wait to see the play, whatever the spectacular that year was. I naturally protested, but he was very firm. He seemed somehow out of sorts about the whole thing. But before we left, he went back behind the scenes somewhere and, after a few minutes, emerged with the teddy bear, as cute and cuddly as ever (I loved him dearly for many years though I couldn't let my friends

THE BURNING BUSH

know how many years I kept on sleeping with him, long after I should have stopped).

And I said, "How did you get him, where did he come from?" And I hugged him to me. But all Daddy said was, in an aside to Mamma, "Well, I had bought and paid for him at the beginning of the week. And they were supposed to recognize the boy and give it to him, but they never did. Now I just wonder how big a fool they think—or thought—I am. They know better now, at any rate." I wasn't sure just what Daddy had been getting at, but somehow I knew that even Winstead's Comedians were not without flaws, yes, even at the age of six. I even wondered about Daddy. But I loved the teddy bear as much as ever and later on even named him Mr. Winstead for the owner of the tent show.

You're Not Going To Die Till Your Time Comes

My father always said, why worry about your health and so forth? You weren't going to die till your time came. And of course that's perfectly true, if you're a Presbyterian in good standing and maybe even if you're not. In Daddy's case, the one thing he couldn't abide was hearing the latest report on somebody's internal workings or their general state of health at the moment, like they were sending back dispatches from the front lines, and very important ones at that.

Not, you understand, that he ever thought you should be reckless with the laws of health; and he did think there were laws about it—not the sort you could create or enact, but they were just *there* as facts which you couldn't contradict. And it stood to reason that if you broke them—by not taking proper care of your body, whether it was too much tobacco, too much alcohol, or too much food, to say nothing of not enough sleep and not enough exercise, sooner or later it was all going to catch up with you.

Now that all sounds perfectly simple and sensible to me and, I suppose, it does to you too; and why should anybody in the world think otherwise and want to make it more complicated? Well, Daddy's strong feelings on the matter probably all went back to his being the only child of his widowed mother and having lots of old aunts and cousins around that didn't any of them seem to have anything else to do but worry about the number and nature of their bowel movements per day and whether they didn't need to go have the doctor peer at some little "place" on their face that didn't look just right, or else they were too hot or too cold or they sweated too much at the wrong times and not nearly enough at the right time or some other such foolishness.

THE BURNING BUSH

Good Lord, don't ask me to give you all the lurid details! I wasn't around them any more than I could help when I was growing up because they were always deciding you shouldn't go in swimming or to the picture show or maybe even breathe too deeply because it was getting that time of year for polio to "break out"—like it was either a fire or else a convict escaping from prison (I never could figure out which). And then of course, they spent all the winter months in the delicious expectation that somebody, somewhere in the family or among their acquaintance was going to take the "flu" and, with luck, "go into pneumonia," which seemed a dim, dark province, like the interior of the African jungles, that few people ever came back from alive, to tell the tale. And a good case of blood poisoning, complete with a hair-raising crisis or turning point, was right down their alley. This was all before antibiotics, remember.

Since I've been grown, I've always been amused by this form of genteel hypochondria and spent a good deal of time wondering what indeed it did mean to them and others like them and what they got out of it, really. Was it just another way for emotionally starved old females to get some attention; or did it have anything to do with Protestant evangelicalism and its seeming distrust, if not downright suspicion, of the human body? Certainly, they didn't seem at ease with what John Crowe Ransom called the world's body and Donald Davidson called the wild particular; and seemingly they agreed with Yeats that one's soul was surely fastened to a dying animal. And they never forgot it for one minute—or allowed you to, either. I always suspected that they began by despising the body as some sort of vulgarity or else an impertinence and then, ironically, almost against their wills, elevating it into some sort of be-all and end-all of their daily existence. And maybe this was how they got their kicks and, ironically, the body got its revenge.

A good Freudian would, of course, say they were nothing but just sexually frustrated and this was the way they took some notice of the body—and in a way that was acceptable to the community in which they lived. Also it got them lots of attention:

You're Not Going To Die Till Your Time Comes

had they had a "good night," how long had they been "under the doctor," were they showing signs of "breaking fast," how was their blood pressure, and, always, always, how were their bowels?

God knows what a psychiatrist would have made of that preoccupation with the most leveling of all human functions—moving the bowels. (A really fundamental matter, Dr. Johnson might have said.) It was as though the bowels, for them, represented the facts of life at their most ultimate, indeed down-to-earth level: life could get no nastier than that. So I suppose it was rightly a matter of the greatest concern for them. Were their bowels "regular," were they "loose," were they "bound," or what? To speak of them, albeit not in mixed company and certainly by no means from the housetops, was, for these good ladies (one inevitably thinks of them as ladies here), to speak of *life, reality,* perhaps even Heaven and Hell; and thus scatology was transmuted into eschatology. Sex, as a topic for conversation, was denied them: they hadn't had any—certainly not to speak of—themselves. But bowel conversation did carry some modicum of social approval. And it dealt with something as universal as death. And on the whole, these ladies stood for death rather than life, which I've about decided is the way the world is divided up, by and large: into life-givers and death-dealers. And these specimens certainly dealt in death. For them, funerals were simply the denouement of the life-long drama of dying.

But of course it all goes much wider than that. Some people stay alive all their lives and, in turn, give life and health to others. Sometimes they're so alive and healthy they're downright frightening; they can even be vulgar, with their excess of life. And when they finally do die, they die of too much life. On the other hand, my old ladies of the eschatological persuasion, having made a life of death, finally succumb to that which has been their life. So in a curious way, they also die of too much life—their own kind of life. But while they're about it—most all their lives, they deal death, discouragement, despair, and other allied negations round to most of their acquaintances—and with a black thumb rather than a green one. Then, too, the discouragement

21

THE BURNING BUSH

business saves them from having, really, to get involved in life, as it is; but according to Emerson—and many others, it's only life that avails, not the having lived.

I used to think some of my mortuary crew liked life better after it was dead, the present after it was past, because then it was subject to revision and correction by their own hands—something life of the present moment precluded. It was more fun, after the party was over, to re-think and re-arrange, then embalm it in the mind, than it was being at the actual party of the present moment: like Kierkegaard, only he thought anticipation was the greater pleasure. My ladies found their greatest pleasure in viewing the remains in retrospect. Then their hands wouldn't get dirty with the life stuff of the moment; and they did spend a lot of time—like Lady Macbeth—washing their hands. Would they have thought life "catching"?

I realize this rambling disquisition sounds more like an essay than a story; yet I believe there's a story here too, when I think about my father and his vexation with the aunts and their kind. He said he'd be damned if he'd spend his whole life in the perpetual contemplation of death and bodily functions. He was as well aware as any man, he said, that none of us knew the day or the hour when our souls might be required of us. But that was all the more reason to live now, here, and in the present. You weren't going to die till your time came, and until then you were supposed to live; and, when you did think of death, it was more as the central fact and definer of life than anything else. Because it was life that was all. And you didn't take anything with you out of this life—at least of a tangible sort—when you left: he would have agreed with Job on that point, I'm sure. His stock response to my speculation as to how much somebody had "left" when he died was, "He left it all!" And further, "They don't make shrouds with pockets in them!" He wasn't opposed to laying up treasures for yourself on earth, you understand; indeed, he thought money and property were very good things. But you ought not to be under any illusions about them—or yourself either. So when anybody raised a question as to how much some-

You're Not Going To Die Till Your Time Comes

body might be "worth," he would always retort, "Our Lord and Savior was bought and sold for thirty pieces of silver." And that generally ended the conversation, as you may imagine. He never would take out burial insurance either; he said he knew they wouldn't allow him to "stay out," though he never specified who this "they" was. But of course he thought you ought to have your will made: that wasn't morbid but just business and plain common sense.

Daddy really came into his own, though, when Aunt Cora, the next to the last of the maiden aunts, died and the last surviving sister, Aunt Ida, asked him if it wasn't the sweetest funeral he'd ever seen in his life—all of her own arranging of course. And he said he didn't know just how sweet it all was, but there was one thing for sure: Aunt Cora, after years of being a bridesmaid, had finally gotten to be the bride; and his only regret was that she couldn't be there to enjoy it all. Aunt Ida didn't speak to him for nearly a month after that, and I suspect that was all right with him too.

The Death in the Dream

I suppose it all started with Metro-Goldwyn-Mayer because I had earlier been taken to see Shirley Temple movies (which I heartily disliked because she was so good, cute, and winsome) and even a bootlegged Mae West performance (seated with my nurse in the colored gallery) which I had sense enough to realize was way beyond me in more ways than one and whose most appealing feature was a snow-white baby grand piano against which Mae leaned defiantly—and I now imagine seductively—after she had slunk across her penthouse floor to make a dramatic "stand" against her lover. But I wasn't up to such matters then; nor was I any more so where the Saturday westerns were concerned: I didn't like all the shooting. Even now a few malicious friends delight in reminding me that I had to get up and leave for about ten minutes during the burning of Atlanta in *Gone With the Wind,* only to be solaced, on returning to my seat, by a contemporary—now a very handsome matron—who lisped, "Never mind, ith's jutht a picthure."

But it was during the Christmas vacation when I was in the fourth grade that I saw the M-G-M production of Clare Boothe's *The Women,* starring, among many others, Norma Shearer as the wronged but misguided wife, Joan Crawford as the designing other woman, and Rosalind Russell as the out and out bitch just on general principles. And there I was introduced to the world of New York, Fifth Avenue, High Society, and God knows what else—certainly whatever differed in every way from my small-town Southern childhood. There were decor, costumes, love affairs in highly prosperous and glamorous surroundings; and I was all for it. I suppose it was my own substitute for a fairy tale: fantasy has never particularly interested me, and I always held out against even Walt Disney, except for a few of the more outrageous Donald Duck cartoons. But movies which seemed to involve real people in real places, living real lives fraught with

THE BURNING BUSH

romance and heartbreak: that was for me. Even as a child I realized my own bent toward the world of right here and now. I never particularly wondered whether there were pixies in the glen, fairies in the woods, or nymphs in the meadows. And I've always been proud of my juvenile reaction to Lewis Carroll: I resented and distrusted the *Alice* books because they were "clever" and, I knew, over my head. The world of three-hot-meals-a-day seemed always to be unavoidable, and I didn't see that there was any real escape possible in trying to slough it off, whether for Fairy Land or Wonderland. Now if you could take this world right here and use it as a launching pad, to proceed off into some sort of romantic idealization or apotheosis, that was all right. "And they lived happily ever after" could apply equally well to actions begun right here, I thought, as much as to anything in the Brothers Grimm.

And such was my response to *The Women,* which was advertised as being "all about men," even though there wasn't a single male on the premises; even the dogs and horses were supposed to be females. And, at the end, a wiser Norma Shearer really did get her strayed husband back, and scheming Joan Crawford got her just deserts, and there was a marvelous cat fight between Rosalind Russell and Paulette Goddard which seemed to settle everything else. So virtue and romance triumphed even amid very posh surroundings. But the next day I had to go back to the after-Christmas letdown, later on to the new year's school term. And I was despondent. Wasn't I ever going to get beyond the blue horizon, to see the sights beyond the confines of my own town and county—farther away than even Memphis? Wasn't I right to hate the world of lessons in school, lessons on the piano, work, duty, and all that it entailed? I moped for weeks afterward, I know.

The same thing happened when I saw an Andy Hardy movie where Andy developed a powerful crush on one of his high-school teachers, and she finally had to tell him that she was too old for him and he must go back to his old girl friend, Polly Benedict; as always, Ann Rutherford and the home folks held

The Death in the Dream

Mickey Rooney fast. And his aspiring spirit could not soar. Then there was *First Love,* where Deanna Durbin got her first kiss on screen (from Robert Stack); and though they couldn't marry for a long, long time (because they were so young, I suppose), at the close, instead of "The End," the final frame proclaimed: "And they lived happily ever after. . . ." And you could just lie down and die because they were all part of some wide world which you could never enter except through the wildest possible circumstances (money, talent, brains, whatever), none of which I thought ever likely to happen to me or in any way be really mine.

Later on, of course, there were the Bette Davis movies, with passions really torn to tatters, and even the last of the Garbo movies. *Ninotchka* I practically wept over: ugly duckling emerges from dreary Russia and falls in love and even laughs in glamorous Paris! And why couldn't such things really happen in so-called real life? Why couldn't they happen to me?

And then came *The Philadelphia Story* and Katharine Hepburn, and I knew I was right back in the world of *The Women*: brittle and hard-boiled, yet glamorous and romantic and of course beautifully mounted. And once more I felt sad; that world could never be mine. Those wry jokes, that mocking laughter were unheard in my own part of the world, which of course drew on quite other traditions for its commitments and its humor, traditions, I should add, which I've come to respect highly as I've grown older. Probably it would have regarded the world of Miss Hepburn's vehicle and the assumptions of that milieu as exceedingly frivolous. Yet I somehow knew they needn't be (a surmise confirmed years later when I made a study of the comedy of manners genre), and again I wanted desperately to escape into that particular world behind the silver screen. I wanted to be rich, handsome, clever, and live in New York or at least on the Eastern seaboard. I couldn't think of anything farther removed from small towns and the South and cotton and mules and sharecroppers. Yet I couldn't imagine myself as ever getting there either. And hence when I saw movies (picture shows, I

THE BURNING BUSH

should say, because that's what we called them then), they filled me with almost as much sorrow as joy.

Perhaps in another time and another place I might have been among the legion of Lord Byron's victims—like Emma Bovary, who thought it really all ought to come true, at least for her. At another time, I might have wept over the beautiful and damned high-steppers of F. Scott Fitzgerald. But I was too late for all that: Hollywood had to be my Orient, my Paris, my Never-Never Land, and like most of my contemporaries, I collected movie stars' photographs and wrote fan letters. (Sometimes I got a kindly reply; had Greer Garson really written that, do you suppose? That really would have been too much, but still I hoped, and devoured yet more movie magazines.) I wonder now whether I looked on those tawdry oracles as received Gospel, even then. Probably not. But it was as near as I could come to the glamor and the dream, and it had to suffice. Perhaps even then I knew I was dealing in a spurious commodity whose fabric would not stand really close inspection. Yet somehow that was all right too; one had to have something to believe in. And New York and Broadway and High Society did, after all, exist; I knew that from reading the newspapers and *Life* magazine. And somehow I sensed that if I ever were to enter that high world, it would have to be through doors other than looks or money, and it would be well to remember that as a sort of slogan or talisman along the way.

Yet I was American enough to be a believer in the Dream, too: it really could be attained if only one worked hard enough. And, in one way or another, a great deal of it came true. I really did leave home, go off to school, even up in the East. And I really did get to New York and the Metropolitan Opera and lots of other places. And I finally even saw some of my dreamer's idols in the flesh. Later on, I even crossed the ocean to see another dream in Europe; and I even made some modest reputation for myself in the wide world of the arts. But that was all much later and has no place here really except to suggest that, in some measure, my dream really did come true.

The Death in the Dream

But I also lived to see the decline of Hollywood as the Dream Purveyor to the World and the demise of the movie-going habit after the advent of television. I saw my Stars, many of them, blaze fiercely, then twinkle out, others merely vanish, leaving no trace. One even had to make an effort to remember they had ever been there. (How much better, I thought, to have made a final flaming exit at the height of one's career like Carole Lombard, killed in a plane crash after a highly successful war-bond selling tour, leaving to mourn Clark Gable and the thousands of fans to whom she had brought such zany laughter, great joy!) But the King himself finally died, Leslie Howard had vanished in the clouds in the war; and after the death of Vivien Leigh, only Olivia De Havilland was left to return to Atlanta for the anniversary showings of *Gone With the Wind*, surely the greatest romance of them all. Perhaps there were other dreams now for other ages, but somehow I felt my own had been all too suddenly exploded, though I had known that, in time, they had to be. Yes, New York and Fifth Avenue still existed, as did a certain elegance in the high world; yet one was always told it wasn't then what it used to be, before the advent of real democracy and the demise of real quality. Had they been changed by the attrition of the times, or had I been changed by the onslaught of age? I suspect it was both.

It all came home to me most palpably, I think, when I made bold some years ago to go backstage to tell Katharine Hepburn how much I had loved her Beatrice in *Much Ado About Nothing*. (I would have feared such an encounter when younger, scorned it when older.) And there she really was, all freckled and rusty-haired, lean and wiry, wearing some sort of nondescript but very workmanlike dressing gown, taking off her make-up before her dressing room mirror. Her secretary introduced us, and I somehow stammered out that her performance was the finest I had seen during that particular Shakespeare run. And then I added, as much for myself as for her, I'm sure: "And I've been in love with you ever since I saw *The Philadelphia Story* years ago." I know it was a foolish thing to say, yet I don't suppose perform-

29

THE BURNING BUSH

ers ever get tired of praise, however awkwardly put. And, in saying it, I felt that I was somehow honoring a pledge to myself, first made all those years ago back home in the enchanted twilight of the Dixie Theater, even if it was only a converted store building with only two exits and a sure and certain firetrap if ever there was one.

But Miss Hepburn rose to the occasion, as both a lady and a star. Graciously extending her hand to take mine, she observed, in that wonderful voice I had loved so long, "Well, weren't you nice to come and tell me so?" And that was all. It's a wonderful story—and has been for many years now—to tell at a dinner party. And I'm used to getting some good laughs and a lot of mileage out of it. (Tallulah Bankhead once put her arm around me and called me "darling" during a backstage visit, but that was *supposed* to be funny. And indeed it was.) What Miss Hepburn did, however, was very kind and very much what a great lady would have done on that occasion, and I could only smile foolishly and awkwardly bow my way out of it.

To her, I knew, I was just another fan to whom she had been gracious. But I felt she was genuinely glad to hear what I had to say, perhaps even amused at the presumption of my being in love with her for so long and from so far away. But in trying to superimpose my dream onto reality, I knew that I was attempting the impossible, and I could not therefore say I was being disillusioned. It was a nice try but doomed from the start: I had known that all along. Yet as I left her dressing room, I felt no particular sadness as for the loss of a dream. I still had some portion of it with me and would have, I supposed, till I died; it seemed something quite necessary, though I had known for some time that it was at best but insubstantial. If I was sad, it was a sadness that went much deeper than the ruefulness of seeing one more illusion exploded. Miss Hepburn had never known — could never know — what she and all her colleagues had meant to me, how far was the distance between the world they acted out and the one I inhabited every day; perhaps their acted world was just as far from their own personal worlds. It really made no difference.

The Death in the Dream

And I think I had known this for a very long time, ever since I had gone out and sadly trudged around the Christmas snows in our back yard the day after I had seen *The Women,* wishing I were any place but where I was then, living in any other context at any other time. Death was not in the dream itself but in one's distance from it. That was what I had wept for so long ago and wanted to weep for even now.

Under the Bluff

Our town is only fifteen miles from the Mississippi River, but we're not in what you might call the Bottom. (Down in Mississippi, they call it the Delta; but we're not that highfalutin—not as much of it up here in Tennessee and not as much money, either.) About ten miles west of town, though, you suddenly come out on top of the bluff; and then you can see the Bottom stretching off for miles in the distance, even maybe see the thin silver streak of the River on the western horizon. You're never sure about it, though. My father *told* me that was the River when I was a little boy, and I wanted it to be so and, I suppose, still do. Because nothing in the world could be more dramatic than coming out on top of the bluff—seeing the Bottom spread out before you—another whole world. And the River *ought* to be there, like an inevitable climax.

And flat! Nothing I've ever seen since (except maybe Holland) is any flatter. There's no place to go but up—like you're at the bottom of the whole world. And the houses are on stilts or even logs so they'll be too high or else just float when the backwater comes, to say nothing of a real flood. It's not what it used to be, though; they've got levees over on the Arkansas side, but just let Tennessee look out for itself—since there wasn't as much land over here to be saved. So that throws the whole thing over on us, when the high water does come. But that's not often now, with better flood control and so on.

But when I was growing up, there was high water almost every year, and once or twice some pretty bad floods—the worst, in 1937. And I remember my mother making gallons of boiling coffee in an enormous lard can on the old coal range for the refugees that were having to be evacuated from the Bottom, away from the flood. The Red Cross had all the ladies in town making coffee and sandwiches for them, and there was snow and ice on the ground; and you felt it all had the makings of a first-rate

THE BURNING BUSH

disaster, like the radio was always talking about. As it turned out, though, it was all rather exciting for all of us because there wasn't any place for the refugees to go except the courthouse and the grammar school; so we all got a holiday from school for a week till all of them were settled around town, to wait out the flood.

One family even moved in up the street from us—in an old house that was about to fall down but the old lady that owned it said it had been good enough for her father in his day and she wasn't about to get above her raising by putting in a bathtub or anything like that. But the refugees didn't seem to mind. They brought their own things with them, including an old broken-down upright piano that, when one of the children wasn't playing on it (mostly gospel songs), the other one was and also a little feist dog named Trixie and a glorious chenille bedspread, with an enormous peacock on it. I'd never known anybody that actually *owned* one of those bedspreads before, and I was fascinated: I'd seen them on a hundred Negro clotheslines, and even on display by the side of the highway for sale. But I'd never really been close to one before. And I wondered what it would be like, sleeping under one of them. Would all those violent colors keep you awake, to say nothing of the peacock, which might begin strutting or screaming in your sleep? I never found out, though, because my mother wouldn't let me play with the refugee children. The Lord only knew what they might *have,* she said; and I never figured out whether this was something in the disease line or else something that might be *on* them, like lice. Of course, I'm still beguiled after all these years by the peacock bedspreads; every time I see them for sale on a back road (that's one more thing the expressways have taken away—roadside markets), I want to buy one and send it to somebody who prides himself on his absolutely faultless taste, with a note saying "I had to send you this because it just made me think of you." And then they could just sit up till all hours of the night *wondering* what I meant by that.

But the refugees fascinated me. The word itself was charged

with drama—*refugees*. I had seen them in the newsreels, in China fleeing from the Japanese, in Spain fleeing from each other. (Later there were the perennial refugees fleeing from the Germans, who seemed to do very little else in life but make other people get out of their way.) But here were refugees in my own hometown; and they weren't fleeing from any enemy but the Mississippi River, though I knew that was a powerful one to have come after you. And they didn't really *look* much different from us, mostly just not as well dressed and dirtier. But that was because, my mother said, they were mostly from the lower element and hadn't had the good sense to get out of the Bottom, like they were told, when the flood was on its way. And they all spoke English, though not the most correct kind; and, when I did venture to talk to them, I usually picked up a couple of new words, which instinct or something else made me decide I'd better not mention to my mother.

She always acted funny about the Bottom anyhow—like everything down there was not what it ought to be and it was all a bad influence on you, like too many picture shows or even drinking and gambling. And certainly, she implied, anything that came out of the Bottom, refugees or not, was bound to be up to no good. I now know maybe why she felt that way: one of the old-maid aunts once told me a couple of my mother's brothers had been mighty fond of going down to Boyd's Landing—which was where you ended up from home when you started for the River—from time to time and having a little fling at the local hotel, which had seen better days but was now seeing worse, what with not much to do after the cotton was laid by but sit around and hoist a few and play footsie with one of the waitresses, or so they were called. And I know for a fact—or at least my father told me—that one of her cousins had been killed down there in a crap game on the Fourth of July forty years ago or whatever. (His own sister said their family just all naturally died young: "Brother" was only twenty-one when he was "taken," she said. But my mother always just pursed her lips and said there was no use acting a fool about it: if you got shot, you got shot, but

THE BURNING BUSH

that side of the house—not *hers*—never did have much sense anyhow.)

Of course a lot of the people from home used to go camping down in the Bottom, especially in the fall; and some of them even had camp houses down there. And it was always fun to go to the River and see if any boats were passing. There were no real steamboats now—mainly just barges with coal or automobiles or something on them, pushed by tugboats, and not the least bit romantic. But some of the older folks remembered when there was a regular passenger service, and you could get on a boat at Boyd's Landing and go down to Memphis or up to St. Louis or most anywhere in the world, especially when the roads were so mired up in the winter that you couldn't get out to town to catch a train. But that was all gone now, with Boyd's Landing just sitting there, and that hotel now pretty much a honky-tonk, and not much else except a general store and a gin. And the River kept changing around so much that, every time you went down there, the houses would be closer to the River because of a new cave-in, or a new sand bar would be thrown up where nothing had ever been before. My mother said that, in due course, all of Boyd's Landing might go off into the River; and she didn't know but what it would be a good thing and the county would be about as well off without it. To her way of thinking, most anything under the bluff was liable to be bad—either unhealthy or dangerous or else some sort of dissipation.

I didn't exactly see it that way myself. Every time we got to the top of the bluff from home, my stomach would all squinch up to see all those miles of Bottom laid out before us. And then my stomach would come right up into my mouth if we drove down the bluff very fast. But when we got down there, I knew somehow that here was another world from the one where we lived back in town. The ground was flat and black, and there were no creeks to speak of, just black lagoons lying lazily in the sun, with cypress knees and water lilies in their midst, and the smell of willows everywhere, and the land so rich you could almost hear the cotton grow. It was quiet: the sun seemed to take the life out of everything except what was growing or just carrying on its natural life, with as little effort as possible. There wasn't any energy much for anything else. That was summer. In winter, it was all pretty desolate, with browns and grays everywhere, and water all along the road from all the rain. (Always rain in winter down there.) And when spring came, you could begin to see the herons and other waterfowl coming down to feed in the shallow places along the lagoons or bayous, and the willows getting green and the River beginning to rise, especially if there had been a lot of rain in the Ohio Valley. And the whole world down there seemed to be swelling with a fertility that was almost ominous.

I don't think I ever thought of the Bottom as being pretty, but it was always more natural or elemental or something than out on top of the bluff, certainly back where we lived. And it always had a fascination for me—just like seeing the River always thrilled me, to think it was draining off half the whole continent. And my father would say, no matter what the folks up North or over in Middle or East Tennessee might think, every drop of water that fell there, whether it was in Pittsburgh or St. Louis or Nashville or Knoxville, had to come right by Boyd's Landing. And that was a sobering thought, no matter how you looked at it. When you were under the bluff, you were not only somehow in another world from home: you were in on the lifeblood of the country itself—the ultimate land to grow things on, the oldest highway of travel and trade. And it was all more like the original country had been than anything out on top of the bluff. Everything was older and deeper and slower down there, yet everything seemed somehow more lasting and more real, the possible danger included.

It was the summer after I was a junior in high school that I went down to Boyd's Landing with my father one day on some business of his. He was trying to collect an old account from a man who was supposed to be making a share crop on Mr. Tom Benton's place. The man's name was Horace Cartwright, and he had a mean name among most people in the county. Nobody had

THE BURNING BUSH

ever caught him at anything really bad, but he had just happened to be on the scene when a couple of prominent men had gotten shot down at Boyd's Landing, and it was said that he always carried a gun or else a knife. He always seemed to have money, too, but not to pay his debts with. Most people thought he might be doing some moonshining on the side: he wasn't known to gamble. And where else could a man in his situation have gotten any money in those days? He certainly wasn't getting rich making a share crop for Mr. Tom Benton, who was about as tough a customer as they come.

I know my mother didn't particularly want us to go that day, and certainly she didn't want me to go with my father: there was danger down in the Bottom, she thought, for my father, and there might be at least contamination for me. But my father shrugged it all off with "I've got a living to make, and he's got to grow up some time." And off we went, in the pickup truck my father used for driving round the county in.

When I was little and used to go out with him on such trips, we would play a game, after we got off the highway and onto the gravel roads, where I would try to guess where we would come out on the highway again when we headed back to town. And I had gotten to know the county pretty well that way. It was still fun to go with him now, though, since I had been in high school, I didn't care to let my friends know I still enjoyed indulging in such innocent pleasures. And I hadn't been down in the Bottom in a long time. Nobody much went camping there now; most of my friends had rather be zooming down the highway to Memphis to a new movie if their fathers would let them have the car. Or else they liked to drive out to the Red Star Inn on the edge of town and order a barbecue after the second show was over at the Dixie Theater and tell their girl friends how much beer they could drink if only they could fool the management at the Red Star into thinking they were legally of age.

It didn't take us long to find Horace Cartwright. We drove up to his house, on Mr. Tom Benton's place; and his wife called him in from the field. He didn't hurry any, just came along like he

Under the Bluff

had all day and whoever it was that wanted to see him could wait if they wanted to see him bad enough. He didn't shuffle either, like people do when they've been up to something or are just ashamed of themselves on general principles. He came up very deliberately and leaned over the window into the truck and asked my father what he wanted with him. My father said it was that overdue account at the store and when was he going to pay it; and Horace said, "I told you last time I couldn't pay you till fall, when my crop comes in. And if you come down here bothering me about it again, I'll beat the Devil out of you." Then, seeing me, he said, "I don't imagine your boy would like that any more than you would." And then he turned on his heel and walked back to the field as deliberately as he had come.

My father didn't say a word. He bit his lip and swallowed a couple of times and flared his nostrils; and I thought for a minute he would hit me, he looked so mad. I'd never heard anybody talk to him that way before, and I wondered if he had either. What would he do? Would he follow Horace back out into the field and knock him down, or have the law on him, or what? I couldn't imagine him swallowing anything like that. And I was scared: his face got so red, almost purple-looking for a minute. And I saw his hands were trembling. Then all of a sudden, he said, "O, the Devil! I'll wait"; and then he started up the truck like he was going to a fire, and we drove on down the road to the Boyd's Landing Hotel. He asked me if I wouldn't like a cold drink, and I said yes; and we went in.

I didn't know what to make of it all. Had my father been a coward, or had he feared more for me than for himself—and not just physically either—and just not wanted to clash with Horace Cartwright right then? But I didn't have time to think long until one of the girls that waited on customers swished up and said, "Now what'll you gentlemen take?" And I said I wanted a Coca-Cola, please. But my father just said abruptly, "No, he wants a beer; and I'll have the same." I was just starting to say that I didn't want a beer, really; I didn't even really like it, though I hadn't wanted my parents to know I had been fooling around

THE BURNING BUSH

with it on the sly. But the waitress said, " 'Bud' for you both, if I know your taste, Mr. John. And why haven't you been down to see us lately anyhow? We've missed you." My father started to say something; but, again, it was like he couldn't speak. And she continued, "Why, I had no idea this boy of yours was getting to be such a *man*. We'll be having him down here on his own for one thing and another before long."

I know I must have blushed, and I know I wanted to either die or run away from there right then. Instead, I just sat there as we waited for our beers, which Gloria (which turned out to be the name of the waitress) finally brought. I wanted to ask my father how he came to know her and when he had been down there at the hotel before, but I knew I better not. She left us alone, when she saw my father wasn't talking; and finally he paid for our beers and we left. I had almost had to choke mine down, seeing that I was drinking it in the presence of my own father, to say nothing of the circumstances we were in. And we got back in the truck and drove off in a spray of gravel and a cloud of dust.

I don't think I've ever in my life wanted to speak to my father as bad as I did then, either before or since; but the questions I wanted to ask were like concrete in my mouth. We drove along in silence, with my father looking straight ahead, his eyes on the road as though it was all he could see in the world. And I wanted to holler or shout or scream or do something, anything, to break the silence that was closing in around us, in that stifling heat, like a brick wall. But all I could get out was, "Daddy. . . ." He cut in almost immediately, though, with "Jack,"—he usually said "Son" but not now—"there's a lot of things that go on under the bluff that it doesn't do to tell on top of the bluff. What happens under the bluff has got to stay under the bluff. And if you can't keep your mouth shut about it, then you'd better not come down here." We had reached the foot of the bluff by this time, and he put the truck in second gear for the climb up. I wanted to get to the top as quick as we could, too; but I felt that both of us had left something behind down there that was very valuable and important, though I wasn't exactly sure what it was.

Where Did the Music Go?

The first music I remember was what I heard at piano recitals. And I've often thought my mother was the longest suffering woman in the world because she took me to every one that was held in our town, always at the end of the school year, some time in May. And I sat there entranced, as girl after girl (hardly any boys: I knew it was supposed to be sissy for them to like music, much less take lessons) floated out onto the stage in her new evening gown, arranged herself and her skirt at the piano and began to play—usually better than she ever had during the year and probably better than she would until the same time next year. I took great interest in their clothes and demeanor, their corsages or bouquets (children love formality) but even more in the pieces they played.

I didn't go in for the "Water Sprites" and "Airy Fairies" sort of thing myself; I was always hoping there would be a Liszt rhapsody or even Paderewski's "Minuet in G" with lots of arpeggios or curlicues or didoes or whatever. I realize now that I loved pyrotechnics, and that's all there was to it. I had a suspicion that I liked Bach too, especially all the voices talking to each other and with the whole piece, as somebody wove in and out of an "invention," to say nothing of a fugue (rarely did anybody from my hometown get that far advanced). But I knew that Bach made more demands on my mind than I was prepared to grant right then. It was easier just to listen to Chopin and Brahms and even Debussy or Chaminade (always represented by that eternal "Scarf Dance").

On recital evenings, the stage of the high school was always decorated up to the hilt by whatever mothers the music teacher had managed to persuade it was their maternal and artistic duty to do so, and usually a handsome drawing room was revealed to the public view, framed by the red velvet curtains, and with the grand piano squarely and formidably in the center. At the sides, down almost to the footlights, were the flowers which had been sent as gifts to the performers, also real live presents, which were tokens of affection or perhaps congratulation that the respective performers for whom they were intended had survived another year of music lessons.

Occasionally, the night was enhanced—especially when the *doyenne* of our music teachers had her carefully selected group (never more than ten girls) perform—with program notes, delivered orally and by the performers—victims, if you like—themselves. And then you would hear all about how, in this piece, you could hear the tiny deer tripping lightly through the forest glades or the angry gray seas beating on the stern rock-bound coasts or whatever. I know one of my friends was immensely pleased when she got to play a recital piece that was full of "Slavonic fire and passion," which she didn't really understand the meaning of, though of course it sounded deliciously wicked. That same group had been previously subjected by their teacher to a most stern regimen of training—as though for a prize fight. For weeks beforehand, they were not allowed to drink coffee or tea, had to go to bed at eight o'clock on week nights, and by no means could attend a picture show or read "stimulating" literature such as novels. That same friend I mentioned earlier confessed to me that, though they all appeared "all right on the night," they were mostly just stunned into tranquillity. And no one dared forget her piece, fearing the wrath of the teacher even more than the ignominy of public disgrace. They sat behind the stage waiting their turns, with their feet propped on chairs opposite, their hands folded in their laps, and hardly dared bat an eye, much less forget a bar. Their performances—and their recital—were always finished works, flawlessly executed, though they themselves seemed almost in a trance until it was all over. Perhaps they were; the teacher may have cast a spell over them. I know she held them in such awe, as she had their mothers before them, that it might as well have been an enchantment she practiced.

Dozens and dozens of such programs we sat through, yet I

Where Did the Music Go?

was never bored. There was the excitement of the occasion, yes; but even more, there was the excitement of the music, some of which I knew even then was better than the rest. Certainly, I knew who played better than the rest. And I longed for the day when I too could glide across the stage and cast my spell. Of course, it wouldn't be so dramatic; I had no wide skirt to spread; and, instead of dropping into a deep curtsy at the applause, I could only bow. Still, it would have its moments as music if not as drama.

My parents, though, didn't really believe I could be serious about it all. They certainly didn't want me, even at the age of seven, "taking up" piano lessons, only to put them down immediately. So, as a starter, I was enrolled in the local "kiddie band," the recollection of which causes me even now to blush violently; and there I learned the rudiments of rhythm and so forth, but very little about music. I finally became an accomplished performer on what must have been the percussion section of instruments, most notably on the cymbals. And my father almost broke up the annual recital, where we performed in costume (band-like uniforms for the boys, crepe-paper dresses and parasols for the girls), by observing, in a stage whisper, that I looked as though I was clashing a pair of stove lids together. And certainly I remember I went about it in a very businesslike way, deadpan expression and all. I had to do *something* to show I believed in what I was doing, even though I halfway didn't. I think we were called the "Merry Music Makers" or some such inanity; but even then I knew—or had sense enough to surmise—that whatever we were making, it wasn't music. Noise, rhythm, or utter fools out of ourselves: that was more like it. But I wanted to make music, and I knew I wouldn't be happy until I did.

And so the next year my parents enrolled me in the piano class one of my cousins was starting—her first as a teacher as well as mine as a student. And she was trying hard to drum up trade, so she persuaded our grandfather—the Confederate veteran—to finance my first lessons out of his Confederate pension. Not many people now alive can boast such a provenience for

THE BURNING BUSH

their musical education, but I can and do. Perhaps, after all these years, General Lee as strategist and Bach as composer of fugues might not be so far apart, and Beethoven and J.E.B. Stuart might even be on speaking terms, where boldness and flair were concerned. But I had to live a great many years of my life before I could see the full irony inherent in the situation and more years after that before I could see the real pertinence in such comparisons. Could Robert E. Lee and Johann Sebastian Bach both have been fighters for the same things, each in his own way? It's a question I wouldn't dare put to many of my friends today, but it gives me great pleasure to entertain such speculations. It certainly wouldn't be the first time that war and music had marched together, the sublime and the ridiculous walked side by side; and who was to tell which was which? Who and which indeed?

It didn't take long for me to learn about melodies; I had been hungry for tunes. And I was able to play a real "piece" after I had been taking lessons only a month. And every time at my lesson there was something new to learn, to build on for the next time, whether it was a new key or a new term or definition, or whatever—really like arithmetic, where each day's lesson depended on the day before. There were also mnemonic devices (or such I now know them to be) to help you remember the notes of the scale and where they came on the staff: F-A-C-E and *Every Good Boy Does Fine*. And there was "snow on the mountain top," which referred to the position you were supposed to hold your little finger in for proper technique—bent just so there would be a small white spot on the joint but no farther. And there were dance forms—the *sarabande*, the *gigue*, the *gavotte* to learn about and finally, after a year or so, a real *invention*, with those voices weaving in and out, talking with each other and with the whole piece itself, striving, contesting, conflicting until the final joyful resolution. It all made sense though it wasn't the sense of two-plus-two but more the sense of another language. And I knew intuitively that, as knowledge, it had equal validity with whatever other disciplines there were. Music was just as real as Latin, just as true as algebra. But, more important, it had hold of my heart and soul, whereas they held only my body, my mind. And I realized that, for that very reason, it had the stronger claim and should be taken even more seriously.

Not that the world I moved in was prepared to do so. Ridiculing boys who play the piano rather than baseball is now old hat, almost passé. But what does the big wide world say to a thoroughly modern instance—a riot at Bayreuth over a new production of *Tannhauser?* The common reader, the man in the street probably has only scorn for such folly. But perhaps, it might be argued, if one doesn't riot over music, there may eventually not be anything left worth rioting over. Man does not live by bread alone, and really I believe it. It may be hard to get the guarantors of the Metropolitan Opera, even, to agree to this, so wrapped up as they are in accounts and ledgers. And yet perhaps they must be so. Somehow it all does have to get paid for, sooner or later, in one way or another.

Yet when all is said, the payment is never made either in currency or in kind. Finally, I don't think it can be bought. One makes music—not as a merry or as a sad music maker—not for any reason but mainly because it's just in his nature to do so. And he has to do it or utterly betray himself. There's no gain, no purpose, no use in any of it, if one thinks along only such lines. I know that used to worry me, when I first started those arduous lessons years ago; where did all the music go when you set it floating out into the room, where you practiced every day or took your lesson twice a week; where did it go when you set it free at the spring recital? I didn't know then; I don't know now. What was important was that you did set it free, let it go, drift, to whoever had ears to hear, a heart to understand. You freed it and were in turn freed by it, from self, from pride, from egotism—humbled, subdued in the presence of that which shadowed forth order, truth, beauty, eternity itself. Your own concerns faded, and you could feel only thankful that you had been permitted to be an instrument of such grace and such healing. And this even when you knew that your execution had been defective, your performance, unworthy.

THE BURNING BUSH

Where did the music go, where does it still go, years after I've touched a piano, years after I've become a listener rather than a performer? Back to the music of the spheres, unheard by mortals, whence it may have come, like some wondrous gift, some blessed vision? Or does it wander far off in time and space, an entity in itself, still reconciling, still healing, in times and places—even worlds—other than our own? These finally are irrelevant considerations, I think. What does matter is that some great mind created it some time, some place (did he wrest it, reveal it from the primal music itself?) and passed it on to us, who hear it and sometimes, if we are fortunate, hand it on to others in our turn. It doesn't really matter where the music goes, I've come to believe. What does matter is that it has been and always will be its own justification, its own mistress: it has no ulterior motive, use, or direction. It's we who try—and fortunately fail—to give it that. The music, in one sense, never goes anywhere; it's we who roam up and down the earth, unhappy, unsettled, unfixed. The music, whatever we may think, abides, waits for us in its serenity, its blessedness—down the long corridor of the years, past the painful, even grisly recitals, the weary hours of practice drudgery and, later, the rare happiness of hearing it faultlessly performed, sometimes in strange cities, in far countries, away from home yet, in the music, truly in our own kingdoms. It's always there, no matter what we do, where we go: that's its greatest gift and ultimately our own greatest joy.

A Perfect Lady

You know, I went down to see Cousin Leila Sue Ferguson the other day; it was her eighty-fifth birthday, and the girls had a few folks in to see her. "Girls" is certainly a misnomer; both Alice and Martha are older than I am—well past sixty. But, you know, I've reached the age when women start calling each other "girls," which of course means that, for all practical purposes, you've all long since dried up and run out of sap. I would say it's about the same as what the French mean when they say that a woman is of a "certain" age. I've always thought that meant at least fifty but maybe even closer to sixty—long in the tooth anyhow. And I reckon *I* ought to know, what with having all my teeth out this summer and having to get used to that. But, like I say, when you get to that age, whatever it is, there are just some things you don't have to worry about any more—even if you did or didn't before. God knows, it takes whatever vanity was left out of you. In fact, I was telling somebody that just the other day—one of these women that her husband spoiled rotten and now he's dead and gone and she ain't got him no more or anybody else either so she just sits around thinking maybe somebody ought to want her (however you take it). Anyhow, she wanted to know wasn't I afraid to stay alone in this big house at night, which, God knows, I ought to be used to, being a widow for over five years now.

And that always makes me mad; it all sounds like they want you to be scared just to keep them company. Misery really does love company, in whatever season, I think you'll find. And they'd love for you all to be miserable together. My sister Maud, for one, just couldn't get over her husband's death. Well, who on earth does, if you've loved them like you should? And she was all for moving in here with me so we could cry all night and both be miserable together, but I wasn't having any of that and told her so in no uncertain terms. Maud never did have much sense; and

THE BURNING BUSH

after William, her husband, died, she didn't improve any. But I noticed, the last time she came out from Memphis to spend the day with me, that she was beginning to put some sort of "heavy rinse" (she'd never use the word "dye") on her hair. And, to tell you the truth, I expect she would marry tomorrow if somebody was fool enough to ask her. Women are such fools, though I say it myself. But then the man that got Maud might have to be an even bigger one, to put up with somebody that hardly ever did a lick of work in her life—worst housekeeper you ever saw and would rather be dead than cook, which is about as bad as you can get, to my way of thinking, without breaking a Commandment.

Well, anyhow, some fool woman I met down at Cousin Leila Sue's birthday party asked me if I wasn't afraid to stay by myself; and I said, "Why, when I get my hair all taken down and my teeth out and ready to go to bed at night, I'd scare Hell out of anybody that came near me, whatever his designs." And then later I thought maybe I shouldn't have said it: I don't reckon her husband or anybody else ever said "Boo" or anything else to her in her life. But then I decided that was probably her trouble anyhow, and she might as well start learning now.

Well, there we all were at Cousin Leila Sue's party; and there she sat smiling and bowing to everybody that came in and absolutely as deaf as a post—hadn't heard thunder in twenty years, I reckon. And I sat there a long time, after I had helped Martha and Alice with the refreshments, and looked at her and thought, if I'd ever seen a woman was a lady born in my life, she was certainly it. And with a handicap that she had overcome more beautifully than just about anyone I'd ever seen. Married to old Hiram Ferguson all those years, and that ought to have been punishment enough for any woman, let alone anything else. Why, child, the things he didn't do just weren't in the book—had a good deal of property down in the Mississippi Bottom, and did well with it but was bootlegging to a fare-you-well on the side. Even used to take one of the girls (they *were* girls then) with him when he made a run down to Memphis after the hateful

48

A Perfect Lady

stuff. Edward, my husband, always said that was a sort of "blind" in case the Law got suspicious; but, anyhow, it showed how much he thought—or didn't think—of the girls. And then he was positively keeping a woman in the house he lived in down in the Bottom—only came out to town for the weekends. And some said she was part Negro and some said not, but I've always thought sin smelled and tasted the same regardless of color. (What would they say up in Washington or New York to that? Sometimes I think that if I hear the phrase, "regardless of race, creed, or color" one more time, I'll positively throw up. Take all that away, and what do you have left, I'd like to know.)

But, you know, Cousin Leila Sue was equal to it. She saw no evil and never spoke any, and God knows she hadn't had a chance to hear any in a mighty long time. So Hiram was always "Mr. Ferguson" in word and deed with her—unless she was being less formal, in which case she always called him "Darling." And that used to make me mad—that stinking old goat and her calling him "Darling"—but I was younger then and didn't know any better. That's one thing being married to Edward did for me: he made me feel he was always *mine,* no matter what he might do on the side. But he was a *man,* and you know as well as I do you can't trust a one of them; sooner or later they all will let their pants down! But, as I got older, I thought it did Cousin Leila Sue honor—the way she insisted on honoring old Hiram. And maybe she knew what she was doing all along—and what he was doing too—though I never was altogether sure about that. That was *her* secret; and, as far as I ever knew, no one ever found out what she knew about Hiram's pussy-footing around. A refreshing change from these times, I must say, when people can't seem to wait to strip off stark naked for Johnny Carson or Ann Landers or anybody else that's hanging around loose. And one thing about it: Hiram died at home in bed too—and Cousin Leila Sue was holding his hand and calling him "Darling" to the very end. And I suppose that was her victory in more ways than one: she *had* him then, you see, and she could make him over into what-

49

THE BURNING BUSH

ever she liked. Dead folks can't fight back, which I suppose is a mercy, all the way around.

No, neither one of the girls ever married. Alice taught the second grade for years on end before she retired, and Martha stayed home with Cousin Leila Sue. But she didn't just sit there and hold her hands: she did more and more of the housework as the years went along, and I can tell you she's one of the best cooks in this part of the world. And as Cousin Leila Sue has gotten older, both the girls have spent more and more time with her. Now at first you might say they've both been sacrificed to her selfishness or something: they ought to have had husbands and homes of their own, it's every woman's right. But I don't know that Cousin Leila Sue ever tried to keep them from marrying, and they've neither one of them ever seemed unhappy about their lot as far as I know. And of course you can't discount the fact that maybe nobody ever asked to marry them: ain't either one of them anybody's pretty child, you know. But, all told, when you've lived as long as I have, you can think of a right good number of things worse than never getting married.

By the way, I saw your father downtown the other day and told him I'd gotten my new teeth in, and do you know what he said to me—that devil? "Agnes, you have had your last good meal in *this* world." And I told him that bad as that might be, I wasn't ready yet to start trying out the eating arrangements anywhere else. Of course, old age, which is all that's beginning to be wrong with me, can happen to anybody, married or not. And I still haven't gotten used—after five years—to waking up alone in the morning. But suppose I'd drawn a Hiram rather than an Edward. I don't think I could have borne it as well as Cousin Leila Sue; and I don't know that I would have had my victory, if victory it was, at the end. There are some things I just don't think I could have put up with; but then you never know what you can do till you've tried—or maybe had to. (Mamma always said that.) And I suppose I'm talking about most anything you have to abide by in this old world—morality or economics or anything else.

A Perfect Lady

So anyhow, I sat there the other day at Cousin Leila Sue's party and thought about a lot of things besides her birthday. There were Alice and Martha bustling around, seeing that everybody had enough to eat (and I'm telling you, Martha made the best devil's food cake you ever put in your mouth, false teeth and all, and all those other little do-dads and what-nots you always have on what the local paper used to call "a tempting party plate"). And they were pouring tea out of their great-grandmother's heavy old silver pot and using Cousin Leila Sue's best monogrammed napkins and it was all done down to the gnat's heel. And they both looked like they were so proud of Cousin Leila Sue they could burst, though of course reaching eighty-five isn't anything like winning a marathon race. People do it all the time and no notice is taken of them. Why, I think you have to be a hundred before you get a telegram from the President or any real public attention. And sheer longevity has always seemed to me a dubious achievement: I don't know that you have to reward people for simply surviving unless they've had something to survive. But then I suppose life itself is a good deal to have survived if you want to look at it that way.

Were the girls still protecting Cousin Leila Sue from some sort of knowledge that might spring on her unawares? Or was it simply their own idea of her they were determined to keep hold of, untainted and untarnished—the innocent, the perfect lady, who neither spoke nor saw evil? And who were they fooling anyhow? I had always been pretty certain they'd found out about old Hiram long ago—nobody's fools, either one of them. In one way, of course, I couldn't imagine life as ever having happened to Cousin Leila Sue. My own mother said she never saw her ride astride in her life. And back when people first started going down to the Gulf Coast for vacations and Cousin Leila Sue took the girls, who were just beginning to have beaux, down there for the winter so maybe they could kick up their heels a bit in a nice, genteel way (and maybe she needed a vacation from old Hiram), Papa said, you could bet one thing: Cousin Leila Sue would never go near that water. He said, "She's such a lady, I don't imagine

THE BURNING BUSH

she'd like for even the waves to spank her!" But even Mama said, after she'd hushed Papa, mostly for my benefit, that Cousin Leila Sue had probably never used the word "leg" in her life and was probably surprised to find out people had them. She said Cousin Leila Sue had probably grown up thinking ladies' shoes were simply sewn to the bottom of their skirts!

But anyhow there Cousin Leila Sue sat the other day, drinking spiced tea and receiving everybody's congratulations and wishes for many happy returns. And, like her usual self, she was asking everybody how *they* were and their husbands and children and so forth—apparently not a thought for herself at all. And I know she didn't hear a word in this world that was said. Maybe nobody knew then any more than they ever had what was really on her mind. And don't tell me she doesn't have one either: you'd have to have *something* to survive both old Hiram and total deafness. And I don't think it was altogether a question of ignorance being bliss with her, either. But one thing I was pretty sure of: nobody would ever know exactly what she'd seen, what she'd heard, or what she knew. No matter what, she was always a perfect lady.

The Sweetest One of All

"This is the sweetest one of all right here": that's what Mamma always used to say, with a hug, to whoever she was talking to at the time—that was only of course if she liked them. And, really, it didn't matter to her or, I think, to them either, to think she was saying the same thing to lots of folks: they all knew it was part of a sort of game. And I've been outside the South enough by now to know that's one game Southerners are particularly good at—what I suppose some big-wig professor might call the indiscriminate use of the language of affection. Like calling everybody "honey," not only because you can't remember their names but also because it just seems to make everything around you work smoother. And even if you really hate them or so much as have even mixed feelings (and most feelings are) about them, it still helps. At any rate, it keeps us all away from each other's throats, which is the main end of what passes for civilization, I've always thought. I suppose, again, it's what the big professors would call the language of polite fiction or something equally silly. But I think it's more complicated than that and mainly shows what they don't know about folks, about life. And you probably couldn't ever *explain* it to them anyhow; they would want to know what was the *use* of it all. And you might as well not waste your breath on that kind of folks, to begin with.

All right, so it is, a lot of it, really a convention and maybe isn't legally binding, like a contract. I don't care. It shows, at any rate, that somebody, somewhere has got a heart, even if it does get used to making automatic responses maybe more than it should. But, when you call everybody "honey" or whatever, you show you have got one and at least you're making an attempt at using it; and that's what really counts, because I think, in the long run, love is the only thing that counts with people, whether in life or in death.

My husband was a doctor, you know; and he used to say that,

THE BURNING BUSH

when most folks came to die, the main thing that was on their minds was who all they had loved in their lives and what kind of love they had had themselves in return. Just as well to worry about that, too, instead of who all is going to get your money or who all you are or aren't going to leave out of your will: Papa always said that when you died, you left it *all* right here and they didn't make shrouds with pockets in them either. And I don't know that I've seen anybody taking it with them to the cemetery myself.

Don't misunderstand me now. I'm not the least bit low-rating money, and I have a horror of ever being without it. But whether you like it or not, the world *ain't* one big Merchandise Mart or stock exchange, and everything on God's earth *ain't* just one more commodity, and people every day in this world do act out of reasons that aren't purely selfish or financial or materialistic. (Of course, your motives are usually mixed: they're rarely "purely" anything.) I remember how mad I got that time Dick Evans, who has done well in the discount dry goods business though he started from absolutely nothing (no money and no background either), observed, about my cousin, George Vaden, that had just died, "You know, old George was a mighty fine man, one of the best I ever saw. Of course, he never made much money...." Like that was some sort of criterion of a man's life and works. It's that old Protestant work ethic still powerful after all these years, you know, though of course most of the folks that live by it wouldn't know that's what it was. And what it really says, though not in so many words, is: work hard, behave yourself, and *you will make money,* which I've always thought ought to be as big an insult to the Almighty as I find it myself. A close reading of the Book of Job is what I'd like to prescribe for all such folks. Instead, of course, I got mad as a hornet at Dick Evans and wanted to tell him that not all the money in the world could do anything for that "retarded" child of theirs that they've taken to Mayo's and Johns Hopkins and God knows where else. (Of course we used to say "feeble-minded" or even "afflicted," which may have been crude or even callous; but then

The Sweetest One of All

changing the names of bad things doesn't make them any better, I've always thought. Whether you call them "underprivileged" or even "disadvantaged," they're still poor folks, as far as I'm concerned. And when you "pass away," you're still *dead,* and that's that.) And all Dick's money couldn't make his wife other than the common money-green-veneered "tack" she was and always has been, even if he has been Superintendent of the Presbyterian Sunday School and a member of the Board of Aldermen for, lo, these many years.

And I thought, yeah, they won't be able to put on old George's tombstone that he made a lot of money but they could put a lot of *other* things which they certainly can't on yours, big boy. And somehow I've always thought that some kind of an ultimate test—what you could or couldn't put on folks' tombstones. I suppose I do have a graveyard mentality: my husband used to say so. But you live all your life in the very shadow of the grave, and it's just as well not to forget it, I feel. But anyhow, I had to remember my raising and hold my tongue and then later on feel ashamed of what I'd really wanted to tell Dick but still be as mad as Hell anyhow. Somehow I've never thought that fair: when you "behave" and turn the other cheek or whatever, you often feel damned if you do and damned if you don't. Virtue is mighty hard to live with sometimes, especially when it involves keeping your mouth shut.

But anyhow, I think everybody has got to have some kind of love in his life, whether it's wife, husband, parent, friend, or whatever. And I think that, when people don't get it—and, maybe more important, don't give it—very terrible things happen to them. They get all twisted up and deformed and then maybe finally just shrivel up and blow away, though not, of course, until after they've often done a considerable amount of damage to everybody else. *Everybody* has got to feel wanted and somehow needed by somebody else—and I don't much care who, which means I'm not strong on drowning yourself in what one of my friends always refers to as "young-love, mother-love, and baby-love." And, strange as it may sound, coming from a South-

THE BURNING BUSH

erner, I don't think you've got to make a lifework out of eating up—or being eaten up by—your family. But everybody has got to find his some one or some thing—and I've got sense enough to know that, for some people, it's got to be a *thing,* like music or painting or poetry—to make him feel that he belongs here and his time here isn't altogether wasted. Which is why, of course, the worst thing you can do to most folks is simply to take no notice of them: most anybody had rather be knocked down than ignored. You know that.

So all right: maybe Mamma's saying "This is the sweetest one of all right here" didn't fool anybody; that's not to say she was insincere or just a heartless old flatterer. What she said was perfectly true in one way, very much so: it made whoever she said it to feel important, feel needed. In another way, it was just a convention, though never a downright lie. But it was a convention that did have—and everybody knew it, in that time and place—very much its uses. And I hate to see a lot of it going now, the more "progressive" and "modern" we become down here. Maybe that's just my graveyard mentality again. But you know as well as I do that the T.V.A. and indoor plumbing or even plastic bags are not synonymous with whatever is or may be the good life.

Anyhow, it all kept the wheels greased; and, like I said before, it kept us all from each other's throats, which, all things considered, is a pretty tall order for what I call the human *animule*. And, really, nobody was fooled or being fooled by it all, except in the way we've all got to be fooled to some extent to get through every day. But, however, you look at it, what Mamma used to say—that phrase and all the others—implied a heart to love and other hearts to love back in return—or, for that matter, not to love, as they saw fit. And, frankly, that's the only view of life I care to entertain. Maybe it is all a polite fiction, in some ways. But just show me somebody that doesn't thrive on it, and I'll show you a dead man, though of course he may be the last to know he is dead. That's always been a lot of people's trouble anyhow, I've always thought.

Wake Up So I Can Tell You Who's Dead

I've had insomnia ever since I was a young girl—way back before I ever married. And I've been to just about every doctor in captivity in this part of the world; and they all just say, well, yes, that's the way some people are and there's nothing, really, you can do about it. And that's not much consolation either: they'll probably all come to my funeral and say the same thing and go on about how they can't *believe* I'm really dead, which won't do *me* much good, I must say.

And of course you don't want to make a lifework out of taking sleeping pills, and I said that before we ever had any of this drug problem business or whatever you want to call it that's coming out over the radio or television every time your back is turned. I suppose it would scandalize the American Medical Association to death (not that I think they'd take much notice of anything *I* said), but I think the doctors themselves are partially responsible for a lot of this foolishness right this very minute—prescribing painkillers every time you stump your toe or bat your eye—until people have just about forgotten that life ain't one uninterrupted shower of rose petals and you've got to hurt *some* just to know you're still here. But I'm a back number, as I'm sure most of the folks would tell you around here. Seventy-five years old next October and buried my husband twenty years ago in June, but I'm still able to kick, though perhaps not very high.

But anyhow, there are a lot of nights when I can't sleep until way up toward morning, and I've tried reading and walking the floor and doing needlework and just about every other home remedy in the world, but I don't want to get started on that sleeping pill business. Like a friend of mine that was always talking about herself and her ailments and complaining about having "blood pressure," which I told her she'd *better* have if she ex-

THE BURNING BUSH

pected to be with us long. Anyhow—always taking pills "to rest her heart," according to what she said the doctor told her. But I just told her she'd better watch out or someday she'd rest her heart permanently, if you know what I mean.

But anyhow, now that I'm living here in this duplex, all by myself on my own side, I don't really *have* to get up for anything in the morning. So the nights I have trouble sleeping, I just finally doze off about six o'clock and sleep till noon or after. And who cares—unless it's some of those fool neighbors without anything better to do than wonder whether I'll be found dead in the bed if they don't see my shade go up at daybreak, the same time they get up themselves? I used to have one woman down the street that would call up about eight to ask whether I'd had a "good" night, though of course I knew what she really wanted to know was whether I was still living. And I guess she had visions of "Lonely Widow Found Dead in Bed: Overdose of Sleeping Pills Suspected" dancing in her head. But I finally put a stop to that and told her I'd call her up myself if I had any notion of dying or doing anything else really important that touched on her any time soon. And that was the end of her.

But God help me, I may have fallen out of the frying pan into the fire because of what I did to this damned old big house a couple of years ago. My children were all after me, since none of them lived here, to have somebody in the house with me. And I never could make up my mind whether they were afraid for me to stay by myself (I don't believe in guns any more than I do sleeping pills, but I've got a meat-cleaver under the bed) or whether they thought that would be a good way for me to supplement my income or whether it would be like having a resident keeper to look after me so *she* could find me dead in the bed instead of the neighbors or just what. Anyhow, I just proceeded to take this old house and divide it up into two apartments and didn't say "boo" to my children or the neighbors or anybody else. But I thought that ought to hold them for a while anyhow. And, just to keep everybody quiet, I had the carpenters leave one connecting door from my living room into the living room on the other side of the house, so everybody could peer into everybody else's business up here and keep an eye on everything the other one did and find each other dead in the bed if it was really necessary. Now you certainly don't have to associate with whoever is living in the other side of the house if you don't want to, and I can keep that door locked any time I get good and ready. But anyhow, they can all come in and find me dead in the bed with very little trouble, if they want to; and we'll all keep up appearances that way. Silliest thing in the world, don't you think? *Whoever* finds you dead in the bed here is bound to be a friend or some of the kinfolks: it's not like you lived in a city and your body had to be discovered by perfect strangers.

Well, anyhow, the first renter I had was little Mrs. Dawson that worked down at the discount dry goods store, and I never thought I'd hear a peep out of her. And I didn't really, and we got along just fine and used to visit back and forth at nights when she was home. But I had to hear all about how she was separated from her husband because he'd stepped out on her one time about twenty years ago. (And who the hell wouldn't, the way she acted, always thinking some man was probably lying in wait under her bed every night to "get" her—she could have put her mind at ease on that score if she'd ever bothered to look in the mirror—and never drinking even Coca-Cola because she didn't approve of "stimulants"?) And then it was all about what "he" said and what "I" said, and she'd never in this world give him a divorce or look him in the face again, and so on and so forth. God forbid that I'd ever tell my inmost private affairs around so promiscuously, and I hope I don't, and I've told my children to tell me so if I ever start acting like that. And knowing them like I do, I'm sure they will: they don't much miss a chance to set me straight as it stands right this minute.

But anyhow, Mrs. Dawson—named Estelle—was a nice little woman, and I was glad to have her with me. And she didn't talk about the time when Horace walked out on her *all* the time. And after all, you can't just read silly women's magazines and watch people getting deeper into trouble on TV serials or even Lawrence

THE BURNING BUSH

Welk always: you need some folks around you, even if they do get under your skin.

And Estelle and I got along just fine; but, lo and behold, it was a year ago last Christmas that I got the surprise of my life about her. After it was all over, I looked back on it and remembered that she'd been talking a lot lately about "forgiveness" and such like and being big-hearted and so forth and so on. I didn't think much of it at the time: in any case, it was certainly a lot better than to have some dried up old harpy boring you to death with what her husband did or didn't do or what "Papa" or "Mamma" said that's been dead forty years and you couldn't care less. But anyhow, Christmas morning—I told the children to wait and I'd come to see *them* after New Year's (I didn't want to be around all that commotion with the grandchildren any more than I could help)—Estelle exploded into my side of the house through that connecting door that I'd forgotten to lock the night before. And there I was laid out dead to the world because I hadn't gotten off till way in the night, long after I'd put the Midnight Mass at St. Patrick's in New York City to bed. (The Lord knows what Papa would say to that—Baptist from his head to his heels—and especially now that they're all trying to talk English rather than Latin and more dangerous than ever—or that's what he'd think, I imagine.) Anyhow, in roars Estelle like a screaming eagle (I used to think of her as more on the order of a sparrow or at least a wren, which shows you can't ever discount the effects of passion) and screams, "Miss Ada, get up! There's a *man* in my apartment that wants to see you!"

And I rose up from the bedclothes looking, I'm sure, like Mrs. Lazarus and says, "Godamighty, what in the world are you talking about this time of the night?" But Estelle sort of ducks her head and giggles and says, "Why, it's nine o'clock in the morning, and there's a *man* in there asking for you." And I was so mad I wanted to tell her to go ahead and enjoy herself and I'd take the leftovers. But I thought that might shock her to death; so I says, "Who in the world is it that's foaming at the mouth to see me in the state I'm in?" And she says, "It's Horace: he's come back!"

Wake Up So I Can Tell You Who's Dead

And all I could think of to say was, "Lord have mercy!" And she says, "Isn't that the finest Christmas present you ever heard of? You've got to come see him right this minute." And I says, "Well, if he's waited twenty years to come back to you, he can wait a few minutes longer till I get my shoes on and my teeth in. So go hold him down till I get there."

Which I did in due course, and it was all just one big love feast. And I couldn't help but wonder what my dead husband would have thought of it all, to say nothing of the children. They all of them were always much more inclined than I was to worry about appearances and what other folks would say. But I just tell anybody that gets after me about that just to tell whoever cares to examine my bank balance: I sure ain't rich, but I'm solvent. And I've found most such inquirers have a great respect for that condition, though I've never sat down to figure out exactly why.

But anyhow, there was Horace after twenty years and apparently not much the worse for wear, and I for one was glad to see him and thought he was just what the doctor ordered for Estelle and even me too: I just liked to hear a man's voice through the wall now and then. But then of course, as I've told my children, that's not reason enough for me ever to want to get married again. And Horace and Estelle seemed as happy as if they had good sense, though he was about the laziest white man I ever saw in my life—wouldn't even carry Estelle's groceries from the car into the house. But they settled down, and he made her give up her job at the discount store. He'd been working in Memphis all those years, and he had a nice pension for them both to retire on, to say nothing of Social Security. So that was all very well, though I wasn't a bit surprised when they decided to buy a little house out in that new subdivision north of town—FHA loan and all that, you know.

But I did miss them after they moved. Estelle wouldn't ever have to worry about either Horace or making her living again, I thought; and I supposed she could put up with a lot if that was the case and was happy for her. I did get sort of tickled once when I was thinking about it all and it occurred to me that it was

THE BURNING BUSH

all like maybe somebody had got the wrong ending for an episode on "As the World Turns," and everything had turned out all right, for a change.

Well, I was not just dying to get anybody else in the house after they left unless it was somebody that wouldn't bother me one way or the other and wouldn't take any notice of whether I paraded around the house in my nightgown all night long when I couldn't sleep or whether I was even dead in the bed or not except more or less to just give the general alarm and let my children and the undertaker take over. But I may have outsmarted my own self when I rented the apartment to the specimen I've got now—Inez Whitefield, a retired practical nurse that came from out there around Fisher's Crossing back in the beginning. I'd seen her working out at the hospital but that was about all my acquaintance with her, but I did think that maybe a retired practical nurse was about as good a one to find me dead in the bed as anybody else.

But I hadn't figured on what all would go with the deal, if you see what I mean. The fact that she'd been a practical nurse ought to have tipped me off, to say nothing of her being a member of the Assembly of God, which is nothing in this world but Holy Rollers that have gotten above their raising and are too prosperous to shout—same pattern as the Methodist Church, really: out of the tabernacle and into the country club, which is at least movement if it's not progress. Of course, the Episcopalians have been there all along (and I'm one myself—married out of the Baptists and into them); so any "movement" they make will have to be in some other direction, which might not be such a bad thing either. But I don't expect anything much from *them* in that line till after I'm dead.

Well, Inez moved in and brought her "davenport" that let out into an extra double bed for whatever Fisher's Crossing connections happened to be lying around loose and her funeral-home pictures of Jesus and what must have been the entire department of Woolworth's artificial flowers, though I believe they're now called "permanent." But what really set the whole thing off was

Wake Up So I Can Tell You Who's Dead

a cemetery easel—poinsettias for Christmas, lilies for Easter—that she kept in her living room when she didn't have it out at the graveyard at Fisher's Crossing in her folks' cemetery lot. I soon found out that wasn't all the baggage Inez had brought along either. There she was at age sixty-five or over, big as a bear and larger than your life and mine too, and wearing pants suits in various pastel shades and with apparently a separate wig to match each shade. I don't know what color her hair had been originally, but it had been through so many rinses and bleaches that it now looked pretty much like second-hand straw. So I thought some sort of wig might be just as well for her, though I could certainly have done without the pants suits.

But that wasn't all. Inez also brought along her two divorces, her "complete" hysterectomy ("ovaries and tubes too"), and a red-hot Holiness preacher from up the creek somewhere that she said was dead to marry her but she was still thinking it over—I'm sorry to say, out loud and in public most of the time. Her background as a nurse of course made one body and any of its functions about the same as another to her, she said: she didn't have any time to take any notice of *them*. And she'd as soon as not open the bathroom door and hand me the morning paper when I was stark naked in the tub or anything else. But bodies dead or alive didn't seem to faze her: it had all been her "calling," she said. And whether it was yours or mine or hers was too much for her to worry about.

So, in a way, Inez was something of a relief from Estelle, who I think always secretly hoped she would have the privilege of finding me dead in the bed. To Inez, that would simply have been all in the day's work—nothing to make a production of at all and just one more old woman less. But she did take a great interest in the news of accidental and untimely deaths, largely, I suppose, because they *were* untimely and unnatural. Inez seemed to think nature always knew best: it was her training, she said. And I used to wonder whether she was a Darwinian out of her sphere: I didn't think the Assembly of God would take much stock in that. And when nature wouldn't cooperate, why you just had to

THE BURNING BUSH

wade in and make it shape up, whether it was with a laxative, a sleeping pill, *The Pill,* or anything else. And she used to devil me to death about not taking any "medication" for my insomnia until I finally had to remind myself that she *was* from out at Fisher's Crossing, where the most anybody had ever heard of "medication" was Lydia E. Pinkham or Black Draught and really didn't much care which was which.

But anyhow, it was whatever happened contrary to nature that really seemed to get Inez started. And she was on the phone nearly every morning to spread the word when somebody she was kin to or had remotely ever heard of (it amounted to about the same thing) had gotten shot, run over, knocked in the head, or just plain killed. And of course she was always right there to get the weekend "body count," when they told you on the Monday morning TV news how many people had been killed across the state over the weekend or the holiday season or whatever and also how: automobile accidents, electrocutions, drownings, even one time a man crushed to death by a mobile home, which I, for one, thought served him right for living in such a monstrosity. And then she would come baying into my room, where I'd probably still be fast asleep, and shriek, "Miss Ada, Miss Ada, wake up so I can tell you who's dead!"

But, morbid or not, Inez does have her uses; and I've been entertaining myself for some time now, when I can't sleep, by trying to imagine various roles for her to play: Madame Defarge or maybe even John the Baptist with a sex change (which wouldn't have bothered Inez in the least) were real possibilities, I thought. But one night last week when I was really having a bad time and was even desperate enough to try counting sheep after Johnny Carson, the *Reader's Digest* and even a right strong hot toddy had all failed me, I got to thinking that maybe Inez was more than a Darwinian out of her element and a wiser commentator than she knew. If she was one to whom both death and life were but different sides of the same coin, one body the same as another, she was also the one to wake you up to tell you who was dead. And what was more important than that: who was

Wake Up So I Can Tell You Who's Dead

really asleep or awake, really alive or dead? (Being found dead in the bed wasn't a matter for speculation at all: it was just a fact.) And don't tell me I'm just being morbid either: how do you know who's alive unless you know who's dead?

It was sometimes hard to say these days who the living and the dead were: what else was the evening news all about, really? And then I recollected from way back yonder somewhere when I was in school a thousand years ago that somebody in American literature—Thoreau, I think—said the only way for a man to get waked up sometimes was to get run over by one of those newfangled railroad trains. (In the case of Inez, it was more like getting hit in the head with a sledge hammer.) How deep asleep you were had a lot to do with the strength of the remedy necessary, I suppose. In any case, I thought, I'd spent a good part of my life (against my will, mostly) wide awake and ought to be about the brightest person I knew. Anyhow, the idea of Inez in the role of an observer or news analyst, giving both the Associated Press and David Brinkley a run for their money, was a novel one and, I thought, about as valid a part for her as many of the folks that were already playing it—and they might as well not turn up their noses at her, Fisher's Crossing or not. To cap the climax, I even began to wonder whether they couldn't make some use of Inez up in Washington and hung fire for quite a spell, trying to decide between the Supreme Court and the F.B.I. I could even imagine her, if necessary, refereeing a wrestling match between Martha Mitchell and Lady Bird Johnson. But about that point, I got so carried away by the drama I'd set in motion, I forgot all about insomnia and finally went on off to sleep.

I Didn't Go On With My Music

No, I didn't go on with my music, though of course everybody did say I had such a sweet touch. Ha! Took lessons for over ten years too, but you can't make a lifework out of that. And then the first thing you know, if you don't watch out, you'll start treating it like a business and thinking about careers and such like. And Mamma and Papa didn't believe in any of that for a young woman. Mamma always said a woman had no higher calling than to be at the head of a home and be the power behind the throne in some man's life. I don't know what Papa thought, but I do know he didn't have any time for women in the business world (he was a banker). He didn't think much of women drivers either, and the Lord only knows what he would have thought of all this "Women's Lib" business that's going on now. But then it's no good worrying about what all the ones that are dead and gone would think of what's happening now: they'd have to make their own arrangements about it all, just like you do yourself. And if you don't like the way the arrangements are made here, well, you just should have arranged to be born into some other world than this. Cut your coat according to the cloth, I always say. And what else can you do anyhow?

But anyway, like I was saying earlier, I wasn't about to get that serious about my piano work, though I still love music as much as ever. And I go in to Memphis every time there's a good concert and especially when the Metropolitan Opera comes in the spring. And I have my radio for the opera broadcasts on Saturdays. (I always feel guilty about not buying Texaco gasoline, as long as they've been sponsoring those broadcasts; but one of the cousins is a Gulf dealer and I own some of their stock too.) And I have my stereo for all my records. So I've still got music in my life even if I didn't go on with it. And what would I have done with it anyhow, in that way? I knew I wasn't good enough to become a real concert pianist (that sweet touch isn't going to

THE BURNING BUSH

do you any good there), and I wasn't about to spend my life giving music lessons to whining little brats with runny noses that were only taking because they were being made to.

Myself, I can't think of a poorer way to create an interest in music, much less a love for it. It's something you either have in you already, by the grace of God or whoever, or something you'll never have as long as you live, no matter how many piano lessons or music appreciation courses you take. Just like old Mrs. Edwards that told somebody that ever since her daughter Emily Ann (the only girl so they all called her "Sister") had been taking lessons from Mrs. Hickman, Mrs. Hickman had taken every bit of the rhythm out of Sister. Well, all I can say to that is that nobody took the rhythm or anything else out of Sister: it never was there in the first place, I'm pretty sure. Like a lot of other things in life: some have it and some don't. It all makes a kind of Presbyterian out of you.

Or if you can't go that far and believe in predestination, you can simply say it's all in the blood or in the genes, like that silly Catherine Barton down the street that still makes a lifework out of what "Father" said forty years ago and thinks your family is the whole entire universe, God included. And she has observed—more like it, proclaimed—on more than one occasion, when I happened to be getting ready to go to a recital or something, that there wasn't a particle of music in the Barton blood. And I always wanted to ask her whether she was bragging or complaining. No wonder she never got a husband: she must have been afraid of polluting that Barton blood. Her own father wasn't afraid of polluting it with that white-trash wench he used to step out with every time old Mrs. Barton's back was turned. But then you couldn't much blame him either: Mrs. Barton seemed to think sex was nothing but a vile though necessary commodity the family dealt in just to insure its survival and you just turned it on or off at will, like a water faucet. I'm sure she would have died rather than *enjoy* it.

Now of course it's easy enough for you to go away from here thinking that's my trouble down to the gnat's heel: I never had a

I Didn't Go On With My Music

husband, so I took to music (even if I didn't go on with it, like they say) as a substitute. And I suppose you could argue that if you were bent and determined to do so. But sooner or later, everybody takes to *something* if life is going to have any shape or meaning to it. And I'd as soon have taken to music (sounds like a drug, doesn't it?) as a lot of other things I can think of. And God knows there's enough folks taking to enough things today to keep all the professors and doctors busy around the clock and then some. And whatever you think of me taking to music, you can tell everybody I'm holding my own very well, thank you, and haven't felt any need for either counseling or therapy or whatever. And any time I need any "professional" advice, you can just put it down that it won't be any fool doctor or preacher I'll go to see: I'll just talk to my lawyer.

But anyhow, why didn't I ever catch a husband, you'll want to know. Well to tell you the plain unvarnished truth, I've never given it much thought, which will probably send you away from here thinking I'm another deranged or even abnormal old woman. Certainly, Mamma would have wanted me to marry, if for nothing else than to give her some grandchildren. I don't know about Papa: he got rich in business by not talking, so he didn't have much to say around the house either. On the other hand, Mamma was one of the biggest talkers in the world, you know; it could be he didn't have much chance. Maybe Mamma put out too much, and he didn't put out enough, where I—or anybody else—was concerned. And maybe I just didn't want marriage on those terms—a marriage like theirs, I mean.

On the other hand, maybe I just never met the right man either. And I'm not about to discount the claims of passion, sex, or anything else like that, though of course I've never experienced them myself. But I think all those matters arrange themselves or not at all. And I can tell you there's a lot of things worse than not being married; and old maids aren't altogether a joke, you know, especially when you're left well provided for and can get a little farther from home than Memphis every now and

THE BURNING BUSH

then. People can put up with a good deal when you're paying your own way, I think you'll find.

Not that I've ever given anybody much to put up with, I hope to God. I mind my own business and tend to my own knitting and try to keep my house in order, in every sense of that word. And sometimes I think this big old house of mine is just too much to worry with, and I'll sell it and move into an apartment. But I don't think I really want that either—just another genteel maiden lady living all alone in a couple of rooms and reduced in spirits if not in circumstances.

But to get back to the music business. No, I didn't go on with it, like they say around here. And yet I don't think I altogether gave it up either: I've loved it, honored it, felt it all my life. And it's given me great happiness and joy. There wouldn't be a bit of use in the world in trying to explain to the likes of Catherine Barton why I've gladly paid twenty dollars many a time to hear an opera at the Met when I've been in New York, but I've never felt cheated yet. People like Catherine don't believe in anything they can't see or say; and if "Father" saw it or said it, it's all that much better. But as for hearing and feeling (and I think for joy too), you can just deal that sort out. They would want to know what the *use* of it all was, and there's no way you can ever get through to folks like that. I suppose they would want to know where the music has gone to after you've heard it—like it was something you'd eaten or drunk or else money you'd put in a savings account. (That's all that kind knows to do with anything valuable: put it in a savings account.) Well, it goes into your head and your heart and stays there even if you aren't aware of it. Of course, if it's been something really great, it may even keep you awake, like a performance of *Tristan und Isolde* that went round and round in my head all one night in New York or a performance of *Der Rosenkavalier* I once heard in Vienna that I didn't want to even speak to anybody after, just get back to the hotel as quick as possible and shut myself up in my room so I could be alone with the music and think about it all.

And, you see, that's what's so wonderful about it all: you can

I Didn't Go On With My Music

hold it close to you and love it and try to let it work back out of you until it touches other people and some of the joy rubs off on them too. But you don't ever *own* it: not even the composer does that. As soon as you start talking about authoritative readings and definitive performances and all that sort of stuff (and I'm not discounting genuine criticism here), you start acting like a proprietor and nobody, not even Toscanini, can be that. In fact, I always thought that was part of his trouble. I never thought Verdi would have gotten in half that much sweat about the way his works were performed: he would surely have allowed some leeway to whoever wanted to play them. Or at least I like to think he would, which I hope doesn't prove I'm too sentimental about either music or the folks that write it and the ones that play it. Music gives you a freedom along with all the terrible demands it makes, whether you create it or just listen to it. I know that much. The real question, I suppose, is how you use that freedom. But imagine trying to explain something like that to Catherine Barton! I'm certainly not equal to the task.

But anyhow I like to think that whatever music you hear sings its way into your soul and somehow blesses you and catches you up into some kind of celebration about the wonder of the universe and the power that seems to order it and move it; and then it lets you go and sets you free, blessed and maybe even healed from some of your sorrows. And you in turn can pass on some of this blessing to those around you. Now that's all pretty highfalutin talk from an old woman like me, but it says what I want to say about the music in my own life about as well as I can ever put it. However you look at it, I know it's given me moments of real blessedness and joy; and I've been so grateful to the composers and the performers and finally, I suppose, to God Almighty for visiting them with such grace. I hope, at any rate, you'll have some idea now of what my music has meant to me all these years and what I think it's done for me. No, I didn't go on with it, like they say; but it sure God has gone on with me.

The Dream House

I remember going to their wedding with my mother when I was only four years old; and, aside from the ceremony, which impressed itself on me as another of those occasions (all too few then) which somehow *meant*, I remember mainly the banks of blue larkspur behind the altar (it was June) and one of my playmates who had been pressed into service (because of some family connection) as flower girl. She never made it down the aisle, though: she got just inside the door, took one look at the congregation, screamed "Mamma!" and ran out. I was very much put out with her: I would have given a great deal to have walked down that aisle, to have been part of that drama.

Of the bride and groom I have little recollection until some years afterward (how selective our memories are!) when they started building their new house on the highway which led south from home to Memphis. But the house I remember from the beginning and came to know quite well: they said it was Marjorie's dream house, she had gotten the blueprints out of *Good Housekeeping* or *Better Homes and Gardens,* and Henry was all too pleased to let her have it the way she wanted. He owned a lot of farm land, was up before day, everybody said, to oversee his hands, and hardly ever came home till time to go to bed. But he wanted Marjorie to have what she wanted, and he had the money to make it possible.

The strange thing—or perhaps not so strange—is that I was never in the house myself. And, really, there was no occasion for me to be there. The Harrisons were friends of ours; and Marjorie's own family, the Davidsons, were old acquaintances. But our families had never been particularly close. O, I suppose my mother might be invited to Marjorie's if she was having a really big party, the way people used to do in our part of the world in the summertime, to get all their bridge obligations paid

THE BURNING BUSH

back. But Marjorie and Henry were much younger than my parents, and there was no real common bond between them. I wonder now what I would have called them, had I ever been in their house. "Miss Marjorie" and "Mr. Henry," I suppose, because, at that time and in that place, such proprieties were very strictly observed. I know of course that, as I got older, I began alluding to them as Marjorie and Henry; but it was as my mother said: when you get grown, everybody is the same age.

But the fact of my having been at their wedding somehow gave them a special interest for me, an interest which I remember, as I grew up, seemed almost proprietary. Perhaps I felt that I had somehow been in at the beginning of their life together and it was all some sort of mysterious initiation for me into the rites of marriage and adulthood, things which I could not yet understand. They were *my* bride and groom, somehow: at their wedding, I seemed to have learned something I had never known before, something after which I would never be the same again. And so their house—Marjorie's dream house—became somehow my house and my dream. It was the fruition and embodiment of something that had happened to them in which I also had been included. And when, a few years later, they had their one and only child, he somehow seemed to belong to me too.

I remember that "little Henry," as they always called him, used to come into town quite often to spend the day with Marjorie's parents; and every time I saw him, I would think, yes, I had been there when his parents were married, before he was ever even thought of—something like that. And I suppose now it was my first encounter with a difference in generations in which I was the older, the superior. And I knew that I had been living and going to weddings before he was ever born, and this somehow made me feel immeasurably old and wise. "Little Henry" was too much younger to be my own playmate; but I often found myself following him, at a distance, as he walked round the square with his grandfather or watching him closely as he played with some of his friends on the playground behind the junior high school.

The Dream House

I wonder now exactly what my feelings toward him were then. I know he fascinated me as a reminder of the childhood I was all too rapidly leaving; but he perhaps also reflected back to me something of the role I was already then imagining for myself—the observer, who can will himself outside the group, outside his own life, to look on things dispassionately and to wonder what indeed they do mean. Seeing little Henry always reminded me that I myself was different. What form this difference would make later in my life, I never imagined. Was it a dawning artistic or critical intelligence? I've often wondered. Yet somehow also it was related to the feeling I had at the movies when the fade-out came, and all therein had their heart's desire, but I had to go back home and then another day of school.

Marjorie and Henry and little Henry were certainly part of the romantic machinery of my life; that I rarely saw them only enhanced their symbolic value. I suppose I hardly ever said two words to them in the years that followed. Yet, every time I went to Memphis, which was often, there was their house, five miles south of town, a palpable image that stood for love, romance, dreams, whatever you like. And I knew I could not have imagined all that—as much of a secret life as I derived from the movies. This house was an actuality, Marjorie's dream come true; and whenever I saw them, Marjorie and Henry and little Henry looked as though they ought to live there—prosperous, good looking, well behaved, "standing for something," as we often say. Their dream had come true; and I had somehow been a part of it, at its very beginning and during its flowering. I thought of them and what they were apparently symbolizing for me nearly every time I drove past; and, no matter how far I went or how long I stayed away from home, they were always there—a sort of unwitting fixed center for me outside my own immediate affairs.

As the years went by, I moved no closer to them; but I did see little Henry growing into the handsome man his father must have been before him (I thought I remembered him as a handsome groom, but then perhaps all grooms were such, like brides' being

THE BURNING BUSH

beautiful). And I gathered that he was going to be as well thought of in the community as his parents were—the usual boyish pranks of course (bringing snakes into the house when he was younger, I had heard) but basically fine and straightforward. But by this time I was living far away and rarely got back home except for brief visits. I did see the announcement of little Henry's engagement, to a girl he had gone to college with, in the paper; and then I read about all the parties and the glowing account of the wedding itself—all written in a journalistic style which, alas, survives now only in a few small-town papers. (Their brides were always a "vision of loveliness," and receptions were always held in "rooms thrown open to the guests," which phrase conjured up great suites of apartments at Versailles but in actuality usually meant only that the French doors between the living room and the dining room had been left open, to give the illusion of greater room if not its reality. Bridge games were naturally reported as always "spirited," and "tempting party plates" were always served in rooms decorated with "profusions of spring blossoms." A high-water mark was reached when one very grand dowager entertained *the* Book Club—it mattered not that there were at least three others—and her reception rooms were adorned with "soft velvety pansies in low silver bowls.") In any case, I read the details of little Henry's wedding with great interest, observing, participating vicariously at a distance, just as I had at his parents' wedding. And I thought I must know something now of what parents must feel because *my* little Henry was getting married.

The years went by, and I heard that little Henry, who was now associated with his father in the farming business, had a son; and I felt very old indeed. But I had hardly seen him since he was in high school: I wasn't certain that I would know him now. When I came home, though, there stood the dream house, to remind me that it all had come true—the dreams, the plans, the aspirations—both theirs and, in some part, my own. For I was beginning to have a substantial career now myself. But always there had been the dream house, as I had driven back and forth to college, been taken to catch trains and planes, wherever I had

The Dream House

set out to in the wide world from home all those years. And it had come to remind me that one could, at least in some measure, have here his heart's desire. Always, too, it was alive and busy: there were always cars and farm trucks in the driveway. The Harrisons entertained a lot; and, as the years went by and their interests prospered, they set out more ambitious plantings—always lovely roses—and enlarged the house itself. Even the dream could be perfected, it seemed. And there it stood beside the quite literal highway of my life.

The first news that I had of Marjorie's illness came in a letter from my aunt: she told me that Marjorie had had surgery but they all hoped for the best. And I knew of course what that meant. But I found it hard to imagine anything could happen to anyone who had been so much more than a mere person in my most secret life: symbols were not subject to the same laws, I felt sure. I heard no more of it from my aunt, however; I almost forgot that danger lurked for the dream or for myself. But, shortly before I was due to go home for Christmas, I encountered one of my cousins who was visiting in the city where I worked; and she told me, with the customary bated breath, that Marjorie's days were numbered: "it" had come back, and now Marjorie would probably not live till Christmas.

Immediately, I felt some sort of terror rising within me; and I had sense enough to chide myself for acting so foolishly. People died all the time; I hadn't seen Marjorie in years, really; I had even heard that, though she was still pretty, she was growing fat. What was it all to me? But there was the dream house, the dream itself. That surely was threatened. Yes, I supposed it was; but wasn't I old enough now to discount such romantic symbols, hadn't enough happened to me to make me realize that this was a symbol mostly of my own devising, compounded mostly of the movies and women's fiction? Why should I feel so miserable? But I did and felt none the less so when I read the account of Marjorie's death in the home-town paper just before I was driving there for the holidays. Someone had written, as part of a

THE BURNING BUSH

Christmas message on a card, that she had suffered dreadfully before the end, that she had lost her good spirits and cried all the time because she hated dying and leaving her two Henrys, as she called them.

I don't think I had ever driven home with such reluctance, to find what I knew I would (and by this time I had been called there on more than one sad journey). For one thing, I knew I would have to pass the dream house; and as I drew nearer to it, I began emotionally bracing myself for some shock, some horror—I couldn't imagine what—which might await me there. But I actually found nothing there on that cold, raw December day of overcast skies. Then I realized that was just it: that *was* the horror—nothing. The dream house, its yard, the garden, all seemed in perfect order. But there was not one car in the driveway, the porch light was on, and the screen door was flung back against the side of the house as though whoever had left had done so emphatically, in the middle of the night, and for a destination undisclosed and for a stay undetermined. And I thought I had never seen anything look so lonesome and final in my life. Did the dream house now mock the dream which had begotten it, and was it in turn mocked by something else?

All during the holidays I couldn't get that picture of the deserted dream house out of my mind, and my thoughts dwelt continually on Marjorie and Henry and little Henry, none of whom I had seen in years. And I knew that, to any sensible outsider, my musings would seem sentimental, even silly; but somehow I felt it was more than that. I had been part of their dream too—and had been all along, and their dream had been part of my own life. It had always been there, too, for me to see as I drove by. And now it was all canceled out by that porch light and that screen door, the soggy December skies, the dead grass, the dormant rose bushes. I grieved inwardly for Marjorie and her two Henrys and her dream, but I suspected I grieved more for myself and for my participation in that dream. Those thoughts never left me for long all during the holidays, yet I was reluctant to ask for more details about the Harrisons: my dream might be further tarnished, completely compromised as theirs and its end came closer. So I hugged both my sadness and my dream closer during that time and even after I returned to my job in the city, knowing of course that time would again heal the wounds, wishing it could not somehow, yet knowing it would and should. Other dreams had been shattered before, and I had survived. But this was a dream of very long standing, one I had held to long after I had known it was a dream and perhaps little else. I hated dreadfully giving it up.

I did not come home again till summer, and this time the dream house did not look so forlorn. It looked lived in, but I reminded myself that its mistress was dead. And I had heard from somebody during the winter that Henry had said that big house seemed awfully lonesome now. I had never written him a formal letter of sympathy: I had thought of it, planned it in my mind—what I would say and how—several times. Yet I had not written it: again, that would have brought the dream and its loss too near. And what would he have thought, whom I had not seen in twenty years and who might not even know who I was? And perhaps he would think it presumptuous anyhow: God knows what he would have thought if I had tried to explain the dream to him and what its loss had meant to me.

One never knows about impetuous actions: they have done their share of mischief, we all know. Yet I sometimes think we lose something of the heart's grace when we do not answer its sudden promptings, and we are then the poorer ourselves in many ways. Perhaps it was some feeling like this which led me to do what I had hardly imagined myself doing, in my wildest fantasies—going up and introducing myself to Henry when someone pointed him out to me one hot July morning on the square. No, I wouldn't have known him: he had lost a lot of that dark hair, and he had acquired something of a paunch. But his eyes were as black and deep as I remembered, and they responded kindly as soon as I took his hand. I am not sure now just what I said—mainly that I was sorry about Marjorie, that I had been at their wedding and had always thought of them these many years

THE BURNING BUSH

as I had driven past their house: that was about all, I suppose. And I do not remember anything he said except "thank you," but I do know he gripped my hand with an unexpected warmth and firmness before I turned away. And I knew that I had gotten through to him in one way or another.

But I could not bring myself to tell him of my dream, which had also been part of his own—something we shared which I felt could never be communicated, something I would never want to communicate either. I could not violate its sanctity, even for him. But was something of this communicated in that warm handclasp? I shall never know. I have not yielded up my dream entire, even though it has been subject to some correction, some emendation now. But I still have some part of it, a dearly cherished remnant. And Henry all alone is still living in the dream house.

A Very Powerful Woman

My first grade teacher was Miss Carrie Oliver; and she had already taught for nearly fifty years and so had taught nearly everybody in town to read and write. But of course back then there wasn't much of anything in the way of rules about retirement—or anything to retire *on* probably; and so most of the teachers just taught on until they dropped in their tracks. They were elected—or re-elected—every year by the Board of Mayor and Aldermen for the town; that was a courtesy extended to the town by the County Board of Education since the town paid for an extra month of school every year. I imagine, on the whole, the board would have been afraid to fire any of them, being the powerful sort of women that they were. And certainly Miss Carrie had taught everybody on the board to read and write and she hadn't forgotten it and wasn't about to let them to either. It would have been a very brave man indeed who told her she was either too old or incompetent for her job.

Miss Carrie belonged to that breed that, I suppose, has almost died out now, all over the country. She hadn't ever set foot inside a "normal" or a "teacher's college" except with a turned up nose and her nearly ankle-length skirts drawn up, as though she were passing through the portals of a house of ill fame, which I imagine she pretty much thought such institutions were. *Colleges* and *universities* of course were different: they actually taught you something and prepared you to make your living or in some other way to be an asset to the community. But the idea of anybody having to be taught how to teach was to her almost blasphemy: *that* was either born with you or you never had it at all. You couldn't, for the life of you, take a course in it. And I'm sure she would have regarded it as an art, not a science. And supervisors and superintendents and such like could all go and jump in the lake as far as she was concerned—and all boards of education with them.

THE BURNING BUSH

Miss Carrie must have been in her sixties when she taught me but no one was sure; someone even said that she refused to tell her age when everybody had to sign up for ration books back during the Second World War. She just put "over 50" in the blank provided for your age, and neither Washington nor anybody else said anything to her. But of course to my way of thinking she had already lived longer than God and probably had helped Him lay out the universe too. Because she certainly knew her own mind and yours too—or what she thought ought to be yours. It would be easy enough to say Miss Carrie should have been a German general or even the Kaiser, but her discipline was always tempered with mercy and you always felt that it was *for* something ultimately good and not just a punishment. I know one time I had to write out "I must pay attention in class" one hundred times, after she caught me wool-gathering when she was explaining what made the sun seem to come up and then go down but it really didn't and why the moon behaved the way it did. And I felt that I had been wrong not to listen to something that explained not only what affected me but the whole wide world, and after that I really did pay better attention.

One time when I had talked during the rest period after lunch, when everybody was supposed to put his head down on his desk and have a dream and then tell it to the whole class, she sent me out in the hall, which was about the worst thing ever that could happen to you: you were being put outside the class, even *expelled* from it. And I was so mortified that somebody would come along and see me there that I went and hid behind one of the big ferns Miss Carrie always brought over from her house in the winter, so they could benefit from the steam-heating. And after I had been outside, I suppose, fifteen minutes and wished I had never in the world said anything when I wasn't supposed to talk, Miss Carrie came out and brought me back into the classroom, but not till she had kissed me on the forehead. Ordinarily, I would have been very much embarrassed: little boys didn't like to be kissed at all, much less by some old woman who wasn't even kin to them. But with Miss Carrie it seemed to be all right

A Very Powerful Woman

and the proper thing to do. I knew she wasn't asking my pardon for anything: I had been in the wrong, I knew that. It was more like Abraham embracing Isaac before he laid him on the altar—something like that, though I'm sure I couldn't have put it into those words at the time. But it did bring tears to my eyes, even then.

Reading and writing were of course the most wonderful things Miss Carrie taught us: even now I still think it something of a miracle to be able to do them—much less teach them. But she did, and it was as though some wonderful code or key were being given you which every day helped you to understand a little bit more of what was going on in the world around you. And she used to tell us how fortunate we were to be able to have such an *opportunity,* which was always a big word with her. And once she even pointed out to me, when I was walking down the street with her after school, a white man I had known all my life and said, "Did you know he can't even read and write?" I was used to Negroes' not being able to do that: I would later on hold the pencil for many a one of them when he made "his mark" as a signature in the office of my father's store. But I had never before seen an illiterate white man, and I recall the shock to this very day. And I remember thinking how terrible it was that he had no more curiosity than not to wonder what the signs were saying when he drove into town from the farm where he was making a sharecrop for somebody. Today, I don't suppose he could even get a driver's license, but nobody worried much about those things back then, during the Thirties.

"Opportunity," though, was a word Miss Carrie used over and over: it was a chance, something you perhaps didn't deserve, that was *given* you—whether to read and write or go off to college or go round the world or whatever else might do you good and make you useful. And you certainly hadn't done much of anything to deserve it, so the worst thing you could do was to fail to take advantage of it. And speaking of opportunities, I used to wonder whether Miss Carrie had ever had the opportunity to get married or was she just an old maid by default because nobody

THE BURNING BUSH

had ever asked her? I still don't know. When I knew her, she had iron-gray hair, brushed tightly back into a club at the back of her head, dark brown eyes that didn't miss a thing (she hardly ever wore glasses), and a long thin hawklike nose. She wasn't pretty, but some people called her handsome. And I wondered if she was one of those women my mother used to say, somewhat smugly, were better looking as old women than they had ever been in their lives—which made me wonder what in God's name they must have looked like when they were younger because they looked like homemade sin right then. The older people who remembered back that far said Miss Carrie had always been attractive looking but didn't seem to be interested in having beaux and going to dances: she had rather read a book or go off on a trip somewhere, they said. Then of course when she was a little older, her mother had died and her father had a stroke and she had to nurse him at night after she got home from teaching school all day. And there wasn't much time for men or anything else.

The impression I got, as the years passed on and I passed out of Miss Carrie's immediate vicinity, was that she had been a fighter of sorts all her life. She fought ignorance and shiftlessness, just as she fought the dirt in the little house she bought after her father died and she had sold their big old family house that had nobody to live in it but her anymore. And it was always spotless and painted at least every other year. And she had her rambling roses trained up a trellis at the end of the porch; and they grew right up it too, or you felt Miss Carrie might "speak to" them, which had always been a terrible phrase in her classroom. Then on Sundays, she taught the primary class in the Methodist Sunday School; and she fought ignorance—and the Devil too perhaps—there. I remember one time when I hadn't learned my lesson for that Sunday, she didn't say much but just *looked* at me over her nose glasses that she used for reading and said, "Young man, you had better get right. I can't speak for the Lord, but you *will* have to answer to me next Sunday." And the next Sunday I knew my lesson. And it was about Zaccheus climbing the tree, and it

A Very Powerful Woman

wouldn't have surprised me a bit to hear Miss Carrie say to come down from there for that day she must abide at my house. There wasn't any arguing with her because, whether you liked it or not, you knew she was on the side of whatever was right and good, not only for you but everybody else, because Miss Carrie had a strong sense of what you owed the people around you, and the highest compliment she could pay someone who had just died was to say he had lived a useful life and been a good citizen, which seemed to have a lot more to it than just voting regularly and paying your taxes and so on. It meant always pulling your weight in the boat, not being dependent on somebody else, and of course taking advantage of all your opportunities because you simply could not bury your talents, however small they might be. Someday, in one way or another, you would have to give an account of them.

The years went by and I graduated from high school and went off to college, but every time I came home I naturally went by to see Miss Carrie. And we would sit out on her front porch and drink a Coca-Cola if it was summer; or, if it was cold weather, we would have some hot tea in front of her living room fire. And she would ask me what all I had been learning and if I had made up my mind yet what I wanted to be and what would be my calling. That was another word she used a lot—"calling." And to her it was something almost sacred, something you certainly couldn't refuse or go back on, once you had discovered what it was—or maybe it had even discovered you. And sometimes I thought Miss Carrie acted like the latter alternative was the one more likely to happen to most folks because she didn't really have a high opinion of their own ability to find such things out for themselves. I used to wonder how she had found her own calling—or it had found her—but I naturally didn't dare ask her. Had she felt she wasn't cut out to be a wife and mother; had she ever missed that side of life? Or had she just been born into the business, Athene-like, from the head of some great thinker and warrior and never stopped fighting once she'd started?

I remember one time she did surprise me during one of those

THE BURNING BUSH

visits, when I was home from college, by saying that I should enjoy youth while I was young; it would never return. And she said, "You know, even though I had been teaching school for a number of years, I never had a real responsibility in my life until my father got sick. And then I couldn't—and wouldn't—leave his side except to go to the schoolhouse, as long as he was alive. And there went a lot of my young ladyhood. So do the things you can—take all the trips you have the opportunity to and see as much of the world as you can. You learn more that way, about the world, about yourself, about life, than any other way I know. And I'm sorry only that I haven't had more opportunities along that line. I traveled all I could before Papa got sick, went to New York and even out to California; but I never got to go abroad and I had wanted to all my life. I still want to, but I know it's too late now. Of course you shouldn't expect too much from travel: the more you do get around, the more you see how much people, everywhere, are alike. But you can't understand that properly until you've learned to appreciate their differences either. But nothing else I know outside the classroom really opens up your mind the way travel does. But enjoy your youth while you're young; you'll never have it again. And you don't know what responsibilities lie ahead of you, the sacrifices and the sorrows; and of course it's a good thing you don't either."

I remember being somewhat startled by this declaration: I had never heard Miss Carrie speak so personally before. And for a minute, it was as though she stopped being my old teacher and ballooned out into a whole round person. But she soon collapsed into her professional two-dimensional self again and asked me what my college major was. But I felt somehow that the shell had been pierced and I had had some sort of glimpse behind Miss Carrie's official self. Not that I felt she was a sad woman on the inside or regretted one bit the life she had chosen—or had been chosen for her. But I did feel for the first time that maybe Miss Carrie hadn't spent all her life thinking about nothing but teaching school. I don't know whether she ever revealed such thoughts to other old pupils or not, and I know that many of them were as

A Very Powerful Woman

much drawn back to see her as I was, whenever they came home. Somehow you never forgot that this was the woman who had taught you to read and write and who had told you what the important things in life were, like telling the truth and taking advantage of your opportunities and living so that you gave a good account of whatever talents had been entrusted to you. And she was part of the permanent structure of your life and you knew always would be: the powerful woman who had had such a strong influence on you.

Miss Carrie finally retired—she must have been around eighty—about the time I graduated from college; and I don't know why she did it even then except that we had a new board by that time and the teacher certification people and the retirement people were all beginning to raise a lot of questions about the older teachers. But somehow I don't think that would have fazed Miss Carrie much: she could certainly have taken on any state supervisor ever invented and the governor too if necessary. Perhaps it was because, as I learned, it was about then that her mind began to fail: her memory began to go, for one thing. And she would get her children, as she always called them, all confused with their parents or even their grandparents, whom she had naturally also taught.

And in many ways that was the saddest thing that could have happened to her—she who had, all her life, fought and fought and fought and then always given and given and given: she fought ignorance and laziness with everything she had so she could turn right around and give it all to her pupils. And now she was reduced to the status of an invalid and then a vegetable. Finally, because all her family were gone and there was really no one to look after her, they had to put her in the state hospital about fifty miles away—what we used to call the insane asylum. But of course it's a lot different now. Except of course there was nothing they could do for Miss Carrie there except let nature take its course, which it seemed even nature was reluctant to do against such an adversary as she was.

But the saddest thing I heard about it all was that, when some

THE BURNING BUSH

of the folks from home would go over to see her, she would tell them that not a single boy had ever asked her for a date when she was growing up but, never mind, she had had a baby the night before and that would just show everybody. And then she would go off into a string of obscenities that it shocked people to find out she even knew. At last, after about a month of this and then finally a coma, she died and was brought back home for a big funeral and burial in the Oliver family lot at the cemetery. And as many of her old pupils came as could manage—from everywhere and of all ages. I was too far off, working in my new job, to come; but several people wrote me all about it—more flowers than anyone had ever seen before and the church so full people had to stand up at the back. And the Methodist preacher based his sermon on the thirty-first chapter of Proverbs, even if that was supposed to be about a married woman: "Who can find a virtuous woman? for her price is far above rubies. . . . She riseth also while it is yet night, and giveth meat to her household, and a portion to her maidens. . . . She girdeth her loins with strength, and strengtheneth her arms. . . . She openeth her mouth with wisdom; and in her tongue is the law of kindness. . . . Her children arise up, and call her blessed. . . . Give her of the fruit of her hands; and let her own works praise her in the gates."

And I thought that was certainly Miss Carrie's life story and indeed her epitaph all right; and I wished she had been spared all those indignities, even indecencies at the end. But that wouldn't have been Miss Carrie's way either, being the powerful woman she was. Someone even wrote me that the doctors all thought she would die days before she actually did: they said that, for all practical purposes, she was already dead then but somehow her heart just wouldn't stop beating.

A Killing Frost

That summer when I had malaria I was twelve years old, and Mamma said there was a lot of it going around and it would keep on until we had the first killing frost. But I knew all about that because she had already explained to me that malaria was something you didn't catch; it more or less caught *you,* from being bitten by a mosquito. And then in school later on we learned that it was the *anopheles quadrimaculatus* mosquito that did the dirty work, but only the female, which I somehow thought was unfair to the male mosquitoes, as though they weren't necessary for anything except producing more females to bite you with.

And the worst part of the whole thing—malaria doesn't make you hurt anywhere in special but just everywhere in general—was the cocoa quinine I had to take. For some reason, they all thought I was too young to take real unadulterated quinine (nobody seemed to think of using capsules); and so I had to swill down that sticky-sweet brown mess several times a day. But no matter how sweet and chocolaty it was, it still didn't hide that bitter quinine taste lurking underneath; and the whole thing was a cheat, I thought. And it didn't fool me, any more than the "specially arranged for small hands" versions of the classics I was always having to play in my music lessons.

Old Martha was still working for us then: she had been my nurse, but after I got older, she just helped Mamma with the housework. Or rather, Mamma said Martha watched her while *she* did it all. But then she washed up after Mamma when she was cooking, and Mamma always said that was the main thing anybody could do for her anyway. Mamma wasn't long on short cuts either: anything in this world that was good was bound to be *trouble,* she said, and there wasn't any use trying to get out of that. She wouldn't even use her electric mixer (and she was about the last woman in town to get one) to beat egg whites with. They had to be beaten with a wire beater with great swishing

THE BURNING BUSH

strokes on the long old turkey platter so as to get the most air possible in them so they would stand up straight. And when I was very small, she would let me watch while she beat (I thought it took hours) until the whites began to stiffen. And then she would make Santa Claus and the eight tiny reindeer for me right there in the egg whites (at least, she said that's what it was). And they would stand up for a minute or two before gradually collapsing back into the formless white mixture.

Heaven only knows what she would say now to all this making cakes with a mix and so forth. She wouldn't even use a gas stove for years: they were too quick and got things *cooked* before they were *done*. So every spring the big coal range had to be moved out on the back porch (it would be too hot by then), and Mamma would use the coal oil stove until fall. And the best angel food cakes she ever made, she said, were cooked right there: she knew just how high she wanted the coal oil burner under the oven. She tasted all the time too, which was contrary to the rule of one of my aunts who specialized in very elaborate decorated cakes but never tasted anything. But Mamma said different people had different ways and my aunt's cakes at any rate always *looked* pretty. Of course Mamma never used a recipe for lots of things: it was all how it tasted and smelled and felt and a little pinch of this and a little dab of that. And of course the result was wonderful, but she couldn't have *taught* anybody how to do it.

But anyhow it was old Martha who used to give me my cocoa quinine several times a day, and she made quite a production out of it—I'm sure mainly to take my mind off that vile-tasting stuff. Not long before that I had sneaked off with one of my friends to go to a big Negro baptizing out at Possum Trot, and it had seemed like a lot more fun than the sedate white baptizings in the Baptist church at home. Those had a morbid fascination for me because there everybody was all dressed up in his Sunday best, yet preparing to get it all sopping wet when he went down into the baptismal pool, which was under a trap door up on the rostrum. And they always sang "Where He Leads Me, I Will Follow" just before the baptizings, and I thought it was asking a

A Killing Frost

whole lot of anybody to go down into that water, with a very good chance of being drowned or at least scared half to death (especially when the preacher put his hand with a handkerchief over your nose as he put you under) before you ever came back up again. And I thought you had to be willing to follow *Him* most anywhere to do *that*. And then I felt bad because of course that was the whole idea: you had to *obey*, no matter where He told you to go. ("Trust and Obey" was the other hymn they always sang.)

But, as a Methodist, I viewed the whole thing with something like morbid curiosity—perhaps like I would an execution, which comparison seemed to be appropriate too because they were always asking the ones to be baptized if they were willing "to be buried with *Him* in baptism." (All that talk about *Him* was rather disturbing too—like when Mama called up the doctor's office and asked the girl if *he* was there, like it was a kind of offense to call *him* by name, *he* was so terrible to contemplate. And when I was real little, I did have Dr. Edwards and God a good deal confused, especially because Dr. Edwards was baldheaded and came at you with that great big shining reflector on his head so he could see to mop your throat.) And of course you knew the whole idea of baptism was that you were going to come up out of the water, washed clean of sin and resurrected into eternal life. But that didn't lessen the horror any. It was like going into the hospital when you didn't really feel sick, then having an operation which would make you sick for a while in order to be finally well. And I was both fascinated and repelled by the whole thing.

Now the Negro baptizings were a lot more fun and a lot more really joyful, I thought. *They* didn't use any baptismal pool but just an old pond out on Mr. Buck Horton's farm, and *they* didn't get all dressed up in their Sunday best just to get it wet either. They all had on what looked like long white nightgowns, and you could maybe even think they might wing right on up into Heaven to join the choir of angels as they came up out of the water shouting and thoroughly at home in the Lord, which it didn't

THE BURNING BUSH

seem to me white folks ever really were. Anyhow, I had let it out at home that I had seen the Negro baptizing and what fun it was, and Mamma had said, well, that was all very well but I shouldn't have sneaked off to see it and it wasn't supposed to be *fun*. And I said well, *I* enjoyed it and the Negroes certainly acted like they did too. And Mamma said, well, that was probably just the trouble, which didn't make any sense to me. But I talked it all over with Martha; and she said, yes, they were fun if you meant by that joy in your salvation and in your Creator Who was also your Savior, and why shouldn't anybody be happy about that? She didn't see a thing wrong with it.

So when it was time for me to have my cocoa quinine, Martha would have a Coca-Cola ready, to take the taste away; and then, after I had swallowed that awful stuff, with Martha holding my nose so I couldn't smell it, and managed to keep it down, she would take hold of me and tilt me back, like she was baptizing me in the waters of fire which were also the waters of life. And I would come up shouting that I had managed to keep another dose down. And then I could drink my Coca-Cola. Neither one of us, I'm sure, saw a thing irreverent in what we were doing. It certainly had an element of saving truth in it: the cocoa quinine was nasty as Hell, and you *were* glad to have gotten through it one more time, knowing too that gradually all that unpleasantness was going to cure you of the malaria, which even today I wouldn't wish on my dearest, deadliest enemy. You just lie there, sweating with fever, then shivering with a chill, and with the whole world's sorrows on your shoulders. And yet you don't seem really to hurt anywhere. And it's all been done by a lady mosquito that can't even hold out against a killing frost.

Anyhow, I gradually got over the malaria, but by that time I had had so much cocoa quinine that I was slightly deaf for a while. I didn't mind, though, because it was something of a badge of affliction. At least if you broke a bone, you had a cast you could show. Well, the temporary deafness was my cast; and I didn't mind using it for what it was worth, especially when it was also convenient—like not hearing the teacher at first when she

A Killing Frost

called on you in geography class and then stalling for time so you could think of an answer but still getting sympathy if you were wrong because, after all, you *had* been sick and it was only right to have something to show for it.

That was the fall when summer held on so long. Mamma always said September heat was the worst of all; there was a kind of glare to the sun it didn't have at any other time, she said. And it looked like the first real frost was a long time coming, and I wanted it to be a real killer too, to put the quietus on all those lady mosquitoes. In geography class, we were studying all about the T.V.A. and what it was supposed to do when it all got to working. And one of its aims was to destroy the mosquito breeding places by raising and lowering the level of the water in the lakes—I suppose, after they had all gotten settled into the old homestead. And so sooner or later they wouldn't have a place to go, and that would be the end of the malaria. And that would certainly suit me all right. Besides, you couldn't just spend all your time waiting around for a killing frost to come. And whether the lady mosquitoes were frozen to death by the killing frost or drowned by the rising water levels didn't make much difference to me. I supposed they had their living to make, but I didn't see why they had to do it with *my* blood and *their* malaria—an exchange I didn't think much of. It always made me mad anyhow when I killed a mosquito to find the blood that squished out of him, and then I would wonder whose it was and whether the mosquito was a lady *anopheles* that was right then on her way to give somebody else malaria. When Daddy killed a mosquito like that, he would just say, "Well, there's another one gone to see Jesus." And I never thought that was irreverent either: it was just a more dramatic way of stating a fact. Daddy was a Methodist steward, but he wasn't about to let that keep him or anybody else from enjoying life, especially as long as you kept your pledge paid up.

The trouble was more with people like Miss Clara Burton, who was my geography teacher and the organist at the Baptist Church. And I reckon she had been there since the Year One

THE BURNING BUSH

because she acted like that organ was her own personal property, and nobody else down there was even allowed to touch it when she wasn't there. One time, I know, they called a new preacher from down in Alabama that they must not have done their homework on because, after he arrived, it turned out that he had dangerous leanings toward some of the doctrines of what we still call the "inorganic" Campbellites because they don't believe in instrumental music in church since it's not mentioned in the Bible. (Plumbing and air conditioning never seem to give them any trouble on those grounds, however.) Anyhow, Brother Whoever-he-was let it out after he arrived that they might do well to dispense with the organ and raise their voices in sacred song with only the aid of a tuning fork and thus avoid the world, the flesh, and the Devil. But when he got that far, Miss Clara said that, if they tried to move that organ (I think she even called it "my organ") out, they would have to move her out too since she would be sitting right on top of it playing as long as there was a breath in her body. And since she weighed a right smart over two hundred pounds, they all thought better of it. They even finally got rid of the preacher too, which old Mr. Escue, who had been a deacon for fifty years, said they ought to have done in the first place. He never had liked the shape of that man's head, he said.

Anyhow, that fall when we got round to the T.V.A., and Miss Clara was listing all its goals and so on, she went into all that business about controlling malaria and the mosquito population. And I thought the class would be glad to know—in case any of them hadn't heard about it—about my most recent round with the ailment and how Martha had literally baptized me through to safety, with cocoa quinine and Coca-Cola. So I volunteered all this information, which seemed to please Miss Clara as testimony coming straight from the horse's mouth. Now everybody would believe her and there I was to prove it, a survivor of this dread disease though of course I didn't look much the worse for wear. But when I got to the baptizing part, she sucked in her breath and pursed her lips and then said I was being sacrilegious

A Killing Frost

and making fun of other people's way of worship and, after all, that was one of the reasons our forefathers had come to this country—so they could worship God in their own way. And I should be ashamed. And then of course I remembered what a big Baptist she was, to say nothing of all that less than joyful noise she squeezed out of that organ every Sunday. And I could have bitten my tongue off.

I think the class rather enjoyed the part about the baptizing, though. And several of them told me afterwards they were going to try taking their medicine that way the next time they were sick. At least it would be different and dramatic, which was always in order if you really weren't low sick and were merely bored as much as anything else. But Miss Clara had put a damper on both my story and my spirits and made me wonder whether Martha was really right about all the joy in the Lord. I suspected Mamma would have been on Miss Clara's side and maybe Daddy on Martha's side: I knew enough by now to know that people more or less fell into two groups on such matters. But even if Miss Clara was right, I thought the Lord might have arranged things differently. Killing frosts were all very well, maybe even necessary in the world outside. But I didn't like it much when they went to work on people.

This Tremendous Lover

I was out driving past the old Durham place the other day (I hadn't been out that way in ages, you know); and they've changed the road all around and straightened it out till you positively don't know where you are or even where you're headed for anymore. I remember George—my husband that's dead, you know—was on the highway board when they went to put that road through there years ago; and old man Fred Durham raised such a row that they had to practically go around his place and not through it at all. And the result was that the road had two right-angle turns that literally took five years off your life every time you rounded one of them, and the Lord only knows how many people went to meet their Maker on one of them because they didn't slow down enough. Old man Fred said it would make him nervous to have cars going right by his front door: they'd just have to go around his front lot, which they did, with those two devilish turns. Myself, I've always thought the old boy would have been a durn sight more nervous if he'd waked up some morning and found two or three dead bodies laid out beside him in the bed, the way the wrecks piled up out there, than if he'd just had to listen to cars passing at all hours of the day and night.

But old man Fred has been dead and gone four or five years now (several years after I lost George, I know); and now of course they just invoke the right of eminent domain or whatever you call it, without saying "boo" to anybody, and they can put a road right through your front lot or your side yard or down your front hall if they please and there's not a thing in the world you can do about it. I don't know why they never pulled that act on old man Fred; maybe they thought he would raise too much Cain, and his family *had* lived on that place since the first one of them came over the mountains and across the state from North Carolina. But I remember George said he was paid a pretty good

THE BURNING BUSH

price for those two right-angle turns, and that ought to have kept him quiet. But, you know, it didn't.

Some folks can't ever be satisfied here or anywhere else: they'll complain in Heaven to St. Peter or whoever else is in charge of what you might call customer relations up there—that is, of course, if they get there in the first place. But old man Fred Durham was made to order exactly along those lines. I don't think it ever occurred to him that his land had been *lent* to him for the short while it was by God Almighty or the U. S. government or anybody else: he *owned* it, and it was *his,* and couldn't anybody ever persuade him otherwise. And he was surely going to take care of his, I can tell you.

And I don't know especially why, either. Not a chick nor child to leave it all to, but he made a big thing out of being "the last of the Durhams" or something like that. And it's true they have sort of played out: all that blue blood may be very well in books and libraries, but it doesn't necessarily guarantee results when it comes to turning out more of the same. Too inbred, I suppose you'd call it; but nobody was ever good enough for the Durhams. They just stayed right here and married each other and lived and died and made a lifework out of being Durhams and "what Papa said" God knows how long ago and Grandma's silver that Mammy Susy hid in the well so the Yankees wouldn't get it and Aunt Jerushah's hemstitched sheets and her "receipt" for beaten biscuit and coming over the mountains a hundred years ago in an ox cart or whatever it was. And they never went to church anywhere else but right out there at Durham's Chapel, and really never even came into town very much, to tell you the truth. I don't know what they were doing out there all that time either unless it was just sitting there looking at each other, admiring their own blue blood or whatever. They certainly weren't amounting to anything as farmers, and their place was going down hill fast enough. They even had to sell parts of it off from time to time to pay their taxes.

Well, as I was saying, old man Fred was the last one of them left. No, he never married—nobody around here good enough for him, I suppose. Or maybe he decided that, since things were playing out for the whole kit and caboodle, he'd just ring down the curtain on the whole outfit. I don't know. But anyhow he finally died, and there wasn't much left in the way of either money or land and some distant cousins down in Mississippi got that. And now they've got Negroes living in the old house, working the place; and they've straightened that road out, until it runs right through the Durhams' front yard—or what used to be their front yard. And if old man Fred knows about it, I don't suppose he minds terribly: after all, it did last his time. And I think that's all he really cared about.

    I don't think he or anybody else in that family ever cared much for anybody or anything else except themselves. No, I don't think you'd call them really selfish: they just weren't even aware that other people had claims and obligations of their own. They were just what most people would call naturally clannish and kept to themselves, and it was just "me and mine" with them all the way. They never wanted anything that wasn't theirs or tried to take anything away from anybody else, but they weren't putting out anything for anybody else either. And I don't think that's any way to live.

    But not the Durhams. They just sat out there and expected everybody else to come see them, to put themselves out; after all, they were who they were and they had been the first settlers in those parts and Grandpa had owned a lot of slaves and Papa had managed to hold on to most of the place. And *you* could just put yourself out for *them*. And that set of affairs more or less lasted right down till the present era. But then they began to die off—consumption, a lot of them. Some of the girls more or less just dried up and blew away—nobody good enough to marry them and they certainly weren't going to encourage anybody to entertain any such rash ideas any more than they could help. And then there was nobody left but old man Fred, and I don't reckon he ever really put himself out for anybody his whole life, from beginning to end. He was certainly sufficient unto the day and everything else. But again, I don't think you would have

THE BURNING BUSH

called him selfish—at least, not right away. He didn't mistreat anybody, and he had a good reputation with the other farmers thereabouts for being fair with his Negro hands and the white people who lived on his place, making a sharecrop. But he just didn't seem concerned with anybody else, didn't seem to want or need anybody else. And after a day in the field he would go home to that big old deserted house at night, and I used to wonder what he did then except maybe sit there and look at himself in the mirror.

I guess what I'm really saying is that I never heard of him or any of the other Durhams ever really loving anybody or anything, and I couldn't see them ever getting carried away by anything, much less doing anything rash or reckless, which I think love demands a certain amount of. And really I suppose it's always fascinated me—to wonder how such people can get through life. Do they really believe that they are all it is, that no one else matters and that no one else—to say nothing of the world—has any kind of claim on them? I've never understood it, and I don't suppose I ever will. Life was meant to be lived, you know; and that means loving and hating too, I suppose, since I've always thought hate was more or less just love turned inside out. (That's one reason it's so terrible.) And it means risking, chancing yourself and yours with other folks and theirs. And I can't imagine living any other way.

I've been lucky, I suppose. Mamma and Papa were the best people in the world, and then I had the greatest luck of all in marrying George. And it was George who really taught me about love; and, dear God, I have had a lot of it in my life. How else could I have stood it when Mamma and Papa were both invalids and practically senile for all those years, and then losing my little girl with diphtheria—the only child I was ever able to have, and then finally losing George? And I suppose the main thing George taught me about love was that it just *is*: it doesn't expect any return and certainly doesn't ask for it. And there's no *reason* behind any of it: you love just because you must—life would be simply impossible otherwise. And then if the people, the folks

This Tremendous Lover

you've had in your life to love, are taken from you, why you go right on loving someone else, anybody that comes into your life, whether they need you or ask for anything or not. What's certain is that you can't stay empty. You've got to have somebody to love: we're just made that way, I think. And when we don't love, dreadful things happen to us; and we become warped or deformed inside ourselves.

I suppose you think this is pretty highfalutin talk from an old woman like me, and you probably wonder who I do have to love—husband dead and gone and no children or grandchildren. Not many cousins left either, and a number of those I could very well do without. Well, I take on a lot of folks—people that'll never know it or at any rate guess what I'm up to—people like old man Fred that I used to drive out to see every week or so, even though he did look like he could easily dispense with my presence, and then the old ladies I check on every morning, to see whether they're all right—call them up and ask them whether they slept well. And they know and I know we're none of us fooling the other: mainly, I'm just trying to find out that they're alive and well one more day. And I go out to the hospital and do volunteer work and over to the nursing home, to sit and talk with whoever seems not to have much company. Sometimes I even go to funerals that I think won't be very well attended. Somebody has to do these things, you know, and I guess it might as well be me.

I'm sure you think I'm a morbid old woman and an interfering old busybody into the bargain, but all this is as necessary to me as I'd like to think it was to the folks I go to see about. Even if they act like they don't want you (and I respect that, I won't force myself on anybody), most of them are glad to think somebody, somewhere, cares enough about them to reach out and put his hands on them. We don't do much of that any more, you know: we just put all our old folks and the sick ones in hospitals and nursing homes. And they just get laid hands on by people specially hired for the purpose, and that's that. And I understand

101

THE BURNING BUSH

a lot of this is just inevitable—modern life and all that. But I think we've lost something, from both sides, here too.

Now I don't mean any of this is easy. Who wants to go out to the hospital and handle the bedpans and change the sheets of horrible old women who don't know you and couldn't care less—repulsive old creatures, frankly? And who wants to go and sit and hear some old bedridden man or woman complain that their children have all cast them aside and nobody comes to see them and they're all shut up in an institution waiting to die, which they are? And then they cry and have a temper tantrum, and you secretly think maybe the children are well out of it all and even age can't excuse some things. I've found, incidentally, that age sometimes just intensifies folks; it doesn't really change them. And if they were perfect pills when they were young, they're liable to be even more so when they're old. Now none of this good works business is particularly fun, and yet somehow it all does do me good in the end. At least I'm not sitting at home with my hands folded talking about my dead husband or feeling sorry for myself and wondering why nobody comes to see me. (That's a false start anyhow: you'd better ask what you're doing for the other fellow rather than whine because he's not doing anything for you.)

And that's my cousin Elizabeth Madison's case, down to the gnat's heel. Sits down there in that big house with all that fine furniture she and her late husband went all the way around the world to collect and feels sorry for herself, now that she's a widow and hasn't got anything but all that furniture. I always thought there was a lot of death in that house even when Henry—that was her husband—was alive. They didn't have any children, and they didn't seem to care anything about anybody else in the world but themselves and that damned furniture—all in impeccable taste, I can assure you, and none of it ever really *used*. And Elizabeth had diamonds too: when she got any spare money, it went into another ring or another brooch. Well, there they were with just the furniture and those diamonds and themselves to look at; and I used to wonder whether they weren't getting so critical and

This Tremendous Lover

finicky that eventually they might find *themselves* not in good enough taste and then what would they do? But it never got to that because Henry died and left all his money to Elizabeth, besides what she already had of her own. And now she sits down there and thinks the world is passing her by that always owed her a good time anyhow, though I never figured out why. Just because she had good taste, or because she had all that furniture and those diamonds, or maybe just because she was who she was and had ancestors the way some people have termites? Well, good taste and ancestors ain't ever warmed any hearts yet, as you very well know. And so there she sits—that could do so much for somebody else (and I don't care who)—and feels perfectly miserable.

But I always go back to George when I get on subjects like this because he was the great lover in my life, in every sense of the word. I didn't always feel the way I do about what all we've been talking about, you know—or at least not this strongly. And it was George who taught me what I've learned—about life, about love, about people. And I think it was George who taught me what I know deep down inside about God, for whatever that's worth. There was that poem that was such a favorite of his and he used to quote from all the time. (He was a lawyer, you know, so poetry and speechifying just seemed to come natural to him. I used to tease him whenever he got to quoting so much and tell him he was liable to end up in politics yet.) And though I'm not really partial to poetry as such, I do suspect it's what people live and die by, in the end, though it would probably surprise most of them to death if you told them: we've all got to have some sort of drama that means something, to think about or look up to, and that's what I think we get from poetry. And that poem George used to quote had some lines that I've come to understand better and better as the years have gone by:

> *I said to Dawn: Be sudden—to Eve: Be soon;*
> *With thy young skiey blossoms heap me over*
> *From this tremendous Lover—*
> *Float thy vague veil about me, lest He see!*

THE BURNING BUSH

None of us wants to love, really; in some ways, none of us wants to be loved. It's such a terrible risk, whether you're Fred Durham or Elizabeth Madison or you or me or whoever. We all run the risk of getting in over our heads, whether in loving or being loved. Yet I don't think we have any choice when you come right down to it: it's literally love or die. And I've had a lot of love in my life; it's the least I can do to try to pass some of it on. That's all you can really do with it anyhow.

What Would You Do In Real Life?

Do you remember old Mr. and Mrs. Maynard's boy, John, that was so smart when he was growing up? Sweet but mean as the Devil too, and all the neighbors wondered how he would ever live to be a man without ending up in the reform school or the penitentiary. He was born, as they say, "late in life" to his parents; and I don't think they really knew what to do with him when he got there. In fact, I've always understood that Mrs. Maynard, who was over forty when John was born, thought there was something terribly the matter with her beforehand and went off down to Memphis and had them go over her in the hospital with a fine-tooth comb. And they told her there wasn't a thing wrong except she was going to have a baby. And she was so shocked or maybe even outraged she refused to believe them; and they said, all right, young lady, just you wait a few months and see. Which she did, and John was the result.

Mr. Maynard was nearly fifty at the time; and when he went down to the hospital in Memphis to see the baby when it came, the nurses all asked if he was the baby's grandfather. And that didn't help matters either. Funny, isn't it? But I think the Maynards sort of thought there was something almost indelicate about people their age even having a baby: they'd gone that long without one. And they were both "sot in their ways," like we say; and I can tell you John was a considerable upset for them. Mrs. Maynard told somebody she'd never even changed a baby's diaper before, and I can't imagine Mr. Maynard was very handy with the 2:00 A.M. feeding. He already had the sciatica pretty bad by then. But John's arrival was what you might call the advent of stern reality in their lives, and I don't know that they ever really recovered.

I suppose you might think there was a real danger for John to become a first-class Mamma's boy and crybaby. But he didn't. In the first place, Mrs. Maynard looked like a graduate Valkyrie,

THE BURNING BUSH

with a bosom like the white cliffs of Dover. And everything else was of commensurate proportions: legs (she still called them "limbs"), arms, neck, and anything else. And I don't imagine she was ever inclined to baby anybody: she had been riding the whirlwind and directing the storm around here so long, telling the D.A.R. and the Friday Morning Musicale what to do and taking no back-talk from anyone anywhere. So the P.T.A., when it came time for her to join that, was just one more thing for her to boss. And she took it in her stride.

No, I don't think she ever really bossed Mr. Maynard; he was a lawyer and a damned good one too—not the kind you send for when you shoot somebody but mighty handy when you need to go after somebody that is trying to do you in with crooked real estate transactions and disputed wills and so forth. And I think they more or less bossed their respective "spheres" of influence, like it says on television when they're telling you about how wrong all the white folks have been all these years, dividing up the land of all the other-colored folks all over the world just so each white country can have one of the other kind to boss. So I think the Maynards did something like that: Mrs. Maynard bossed the home, and Mr. Maynard bossed the office. And the rest was just an armed truce. And they had their lives all neatly arranged and, I'm sure, expected to do the same thing with death, when it finally arrived. But instead of death, they got John; and I expect there were times when they thought that was worse.

Riding his tricycle through Mrs. Maynard's petunia beds and turpentining her favorite Persian cat (named Patricia Ann) were just all in a day's work to him. And roller-skating down the halls of his father's office building wasn't anything out of the ordinary either. But it was real funny because, in a way, both Mr. and Mrs. Maynard sort of liked it, after they got used to it. They had both been settled in such a nice comfortable rut for so long; and whatever else John did, he got them out of that and made them sit up and take notice of the big wide world outside. Of course, I think they were still sort of puzzled by it after they'd seen it. (You can't imagine how it looked to see old Mr. Maynard, looking as dignified as a successful undertaker, taking John by the hand and leading him, kicking and screaming all the while, firmly into the Methodist Sunday School. But that wasn't any stranger than Mrs. Maynard going over, in state, you might say—best crepe dress and her pearls—to talk to John's teacher after he had emptied his ink bottle into the goldfish bowl in the third grade.)

But I think they really sort of liked it, though I don't think they ever really got used to it in the sense of understanding that that was what you could expect from a boy like that—the unexpected. They always acted sort of *puzzled* about him, not worried or annoyed or anything like that: just puzzled. And I wondered if they hadn't really felt that way when they found out Mrs. Maynard was pregnant in the first place: I don't think any of it was on their program, by any manner of means, but they were willing to go along for the ride—like a *National Geographic* excursion into darkest Africa or the uncharted seas of Antarctica or somewhere. Like I said before, though, I think it was actually reality that was catching up with them, though naturally they couldn't know that at the time.

Not of course that Mrs. Maynard's life was materially affected: she didn't sink into the homebody-housewife with horizons no farther away than the pitter-patter of tiny feet and what the Avon lady had told her the last time she came round. (That *is* death, you know—when somebody says, "My Avon lady told me so-and-so." The only thing worse that I can think of is for somebody to announce, as though giving the final word on life and death, "Well, I read an article in the *Reader's Digest* that said. . . ." When you get to that level, you're done for, I've always thought. I doubt if even Dr. Norman Vincent Peale could bring you back, to say nothing of Mary Baker Eddy.) But I'm sure her life had an added dimension to it, after John came—just like Mr. Maynard, rheumatism and all, going on an overnight camping trip with the Boy Scouts when John was one and almost ending up a real live first-aid case for them to work on before it was over.

But the funny thing—thank the Lord—was that John did live

THE BURNING BUSH

to grow up; and I'm happy to say he's done real well. Got a Ph.D. degree and teaches history at the state university. I reckon that, way down deep, he had something in him that came from both sides of the house. Whatever else they were, both Mr. and Mrs. Maynard were never down-and-outers. *Indomitable* was just naturally a word that always came to mind when you thought of them. Now I think it's entirely possible that John held them at arm's length while he was growing up, not because they would eat him up alive with affection but maybe because he wasn't sure what to do with them, they were so much older than he was. And I don't *know* this, but I think maybe he was somehow ashamed of them—for having him so late in the day, like he was the product of old people's lust or their worn out sexuality, which they apparently didn't understand or they would never have been caught out and had him in the first place. And the whole thing was somehow improper or inappropriate.

Now he never said anything about this to me in so many words, and we saw him every day of the world as he walked by our house on the way to school. And my husband was his Scoutmaster. But I know he seemed to enjoy coming down to see us, what with all the children running wild through the house and generally upsetting the ways of daily life, which of course is what they're supposed to do anyhow, if you have them in the first place. If you aren't prepared for that, you'd better let well enough alone. And remember, they're not responsible for being here. Anyhow, our house was probably a change from the peace and quiet at home; and he could holler and scream and run wild with the best of them. I know one time I was real touched, when John was about twelve, when he told me he wished like anything his parents were young enough to go to the dance my husband and I were going to at the Country Club. And then he said: "Why I reckon they don't even have ugly thoughts any more. They certainly don't smoke or drink." I don't know what he meant by "ugly thoughts," but I suppose it had something to do with sex. What else?

Years later, he used to joke about the whole thing. And I

What Would You Do in Real Life?

know one time, when he came down to see us when he was home from college, he told us a tale somebody had told him about the day he was born. Someone brought the news in to Morrison's Drug Store down on the square—that the Maynards had a fine eight-pound son. And Mr. Morrison, who was filling a prescription for old Mrs. Jenkins' chronic biliousness, which it was no wonder she had, eating everything that would lie still—and at the age of eighty-five too, spoke up and said, "Well, that's something of a surprise, but anyhow it will certainly be the last one for them." But old Abner Crockett, who always got there by eight o'clock so he could start his day's work of keeping the chair bottom warm back by the prescription counter where he could talk to everybody that came in and ask them about their ailments before going on to describe the latest symptoms he had had in the middle of the night, said, "Well, you never know. You get some of these old clocks wound up, and they never will run down!" And John laughed like anything when he came to the end of the story, but I wondered even then if he still wasn't somehow hurt by the whole thing—what the old man had said—but, maybe more so, by the embarrassment of being born out of season, as you might say.

Whatever it did to him—having those older parents who were nevertheless pretty firm with him, it certainly made him into a fine man, though. And I guess it gave him about as good an initiation into reality as you can have, though, for John, it all started pretty early. After all, *he* had been something of an initiation for his parents. All his life he was around folks that were either dead or dying or else old people with very strong wills and no time for any foolishness out of the young. And though he always seemed to like being around the younger folks, somehow I think he felt more really at ease with the older ones, which, I suppose, was to be expected. Reality started *happening* to him early too: both Mr. and Mrs. Maynard died before he was thirty—and both of them after lingering illnesses. And so John had to go through some things in his twenties that many folks don't have to cope with till they're fifty. And I can tell you, it'll make a Christian and a man of you; and I say that from having

109

THE BURNING BUSH

hired and fired enough nurses to look after Mamma and Papa, when they got old, to stretch from here to Memphis. (You can get somebody for a while; but if they're so perfect they start to sprout wings, they still get tired of it. And if they want to walk out on you in the middle of the night, there's not a damned thing you can do about it but start looking for somebody else. It takes twenty-four-hour supervision, and then of course *you* have to supervise the supervisor. I hate to think we're all coming to nursing homes in the end, but I don't see any way out of it myself. The day of taking care of your sick folks in your own home has just about *gone with the wind*.)

Anyhow, John got initiated pretty early into the harsh realities, or whatever you want to call them. And I don't think he ever had much time for people that hadn't learned about them along the way. Of course some people seem to be able to do that; but then they seem to be living on some kind of capital—like "what Papa said," which really means "what Papa left," or else "My mother was a Lee" or something else equally silly. There ain't going to be any notice taken of that at the bank, I can tell you—or, for that matter, in the Great Beyond. Anyhow, John used to come and see me real often after he went to work teaching. Now that Mr. and Mrs. Maynard are gone, he naturally doesn't come home so much, though of course he still has some property here. But you can look after that from a distance pretty easily these days, especially if it's farm land (which you aren't really making anything off of anyhow), and you just have the bank send you the gin receipts and pay the taxes regularly and try to hold on to good renters if you're lucky enough to get them.

Wherever he got it and however he got it, John still seems to have a pretty good grip on reality, which must be a refreshing change from some of the folks he has to work with at the University, if what he says about them is so. Fight like cats in a swill pail all the time and couldn't care less about *what* they're teaching but just how far they can get their feet in the trough and how far removed from the scene they can be when it's time for any real work to be done. And expect to be subsidized with a grant or a

What Would You Do in Real Life?

fellowship or whatever practically to go to the bathroom. I know one time I heard him say that, every now and then, he longed just to take some of that sort of folks into a private room and whisper into their ears, like he was telling them the real facts of life (which of course he would be), and ask them whether they had heard about sin and death and disease and double-entry bookkeeping. And he said some of them would probably be just as shocked as their grandmothers had been when they learned the "facts of life" on their wedding night, or earlier if they were lucky.

But the thing I always remember best is John telling about asking some real jackass—maybe a Dean or somebody high up but it doesn't matter because most of them sound like they're made in the same mold—what he would do about something if he was in *real life,* meaning, I suppose, anything outside the academic world. And of course the other fellow didn't like it a bit because it made whatever he was doing sound of no importance and all a tempest in a teapot, which I suspect it probably was. Anyhow, that tale has had a right strong effect on me, in one way or another, because, when you come right down to it, half the people you know are probably *not* living in real life but in whatever other world they've made for themselves or buried their heads in, like an ostrich with his head in the sand. And whether it's "what Papa said" or "Mamma was a Lee" or "You know, Grandfather was a Senator or a Bishop" or God knows what—a bank robber, for all I care—doesn't really make much difference. For that matter, there've been times when I wasn't sure just how far apart those last three occupations really were. The main thing is that you ain't done a damn bit of it yourself: you're just trading on somebody else's work and spending their capital. And you can't make a lifework out of that. Sooner or later, you do have to live in real life.

And I reckon that's something John Maynard learned a long time ago. Lucky he did early in the day, though of course you can always get sentimental about it and think the "facts of life" ought to be shrouded in mystery as long as possible, and then

THE BURNING BUSH

bemoan the loss of innocence and so forth when the time of revelation finally does arrive, as it always does for most people. Some silly folks do seem to go nearly all their lives without having to come to terms with such matters, but then I'm just callous enough—or spiteful enough—to think it's their loss. It's a right sobering but finally a right rewarding question to stop and ask yourself every now and then: what would you do in real life? And whatever he may have been like as a youngster, I'm still inclined to think John Maynard has learned the answer to that question pretty well and turned out to be one of the sanest—and most unsettling—people I know. I'm real proud of him.

A Peacock on a Sparrow's Back

When I was a little boy, my father used to sing me to sleep with a lot of the old songs and rhymes he had heard from his father, who had grown up in Virginia, then fought for the Confederacy, and, when all was over and his fortunes were as devastated as Virginia's, had migrated to Tennessee. I don't know whether Pa, as all the family called him, was ever really reconstructed or not; perhaps, like General Lee himself, he took a higher tone than most and always referred to the enemy as "those people over there." But he was a man of very strong convictions about politics and religion and most every other topic necessary for one's health and spiritual well-being. And you couldn't have changed his mind with a sledgehammer, once he got it set.

Pa never missed a Confederate reunion that he could get the money to go to, and today I still have in my possession a photograph of him and the most beloved colored man in our town, all dressed up before they boarded the train for Richmond and another reunion. I've often wondered, indeed, what many of my liberal friends, both South and North, would say to this photograph. The colored man was of course always called "Uncle" Johnny—a courtesy title—and I'm sure he was patronized by the white community. But he had fought for the Confederacy—as his master's body servant—and was as loyal a Southerner as one could imagine. Today, of course, Uncle Johnny would be written off as an Uncle Tom; God knows what they would do with Pa, except that I don't believe anybody, anywhere could ever have written him off as anything. If you couldn't write him off, you couldn't write him down either: he was nobody's statistic.

My own father was somewhat different. He had seen his father, born with servants (never called "slaves") to wait on him and not really ever planning to make any change, married to my grandmother, whose little "place"—hardly big enough to be called a real farm—was all that stood between them and starva-

THE BURNING BUSH

tion, and content to follow the line of least resistance. It was naturally easier to sit around telling tales and recalling old times than it was to be up and doing. Whether my grandmother, who died long before I was born, ever resented this state of affairs, I don't know: she seems to have spent all her waking hours cooking, washing, ironing, raising her five boys and two girls, and apparently leading an utterly selfless life. I know, shortly after my father and mother were married, he firmly took down the clothesline she had installed in the back yard and said he never in the world wanted to see her washing or ironing either and that if it hadn't been for that sort of thing, his mother would have been alive that very day. His youngest brother, my uncle, whom he adored, said that my grandmother had died of grief: their youngest sister, who was so beautiful and apparently a model of Christian young womanhood, as understood in those days, had died the preceding summer, and Grandma never recovered from her loss. I used to wonder whether my father's and my uncle's respective explanations weren't but two sides of the same coin. Their life was hard, the times were hard—certainly for small cotton farmers in the South; yet they were happy as a family and remained clannish or, as we still say, "real close," all their lives. Their father, Pa, provided the history, the background; and Grandma provided the land and the sweat. Whether they ever resented what seemed Pa's apparent failure to make a good living, I never knew: he was their father and as such commanded—and received—their respect. But they loved their mother—and very deeply: I could tell that.

But one of those old Virginia songs Daddy used to sing to me at night had a wonderful verse that went like this:

> *A peacock sitting on a sparrow's back;*
> *A sparrow trying to crow;*
> *A dead man trying to shape a shoe;*
> *A blind man trying to sew.*

And it sounded wonderful and awful at the same time. Peacocks

A Peacock on a Sparrow's Back

I knew, from some friends of ours who had a sure-enough stately home out on the edge of town, with real peacocks parading regally on the front lawn—just like in *Gone With the Wind*. And they alternately delighted and awed me, with their pompous struttings, shrill cries, and glorious spread tails—spread of course only when it suited them—a beguiling mystery yet one not too remote or fearful. Indeed, it was something like the night-blooming cereus I was taken by my nurse to see, one summer night about ten o'clock, when ordinarily I would have been in bed. It bloomed only once a year; and some neighbors up the street—an elderly couple with a plain house and, I imagine, equally plain minds—regarded it as their chief treasure, which it probably was. The plant was firmly ensconced in a washtub on their front porch, in the very place of public honor; and we had flashlights to see the enormous buds unfold and reveal the beauty and glory inside—the Nativity scene, I was told, complete with the Manger and the Baby Jesus, represented in what I was much later to learn was really the sexual organs of the plant.

By the time I was old enough to learn that, though, I had seen many other childhood mysteries crumble and even disappear in the light of common day, at the mere touch of cold philosophy. Yet I had found also that other mysteries, other charms might very well come to take their places. I had learned that the old verse Daddy had sung to me was probably a snatch from some long wandering riddle song—perhaps even from one variant of a Child ballad, in which a series of impossible tasks was imposed on another by someone seeking the mastery over him. But altogether impossible? Yes and no. Sparrows didn't crow, yet I had heard one of the local patriarchs say that the Murrays (a very prolific local family) and the English sparrows were about to take over the whole town. Something to crow about indeed. Dead men couldn't rise again—at least in the present order of things; yet I had learned that the people you had loved—and hated, though long dead and gone, might be more alive in the present than you thought. And I had seen the blind often "seeing" more with no eyes than many "sighted" persons.

THE BURNING BUSH

The longer one lived, the more he came to see that, in some ways, the fewer real impossibilities there were, the fuzzier the lines became between right and wrong, delight and despair, the plain and the wonderful, Pa and Grandma, even Pa and Uncle Johnny. Was that what growing up was all about—seeing that the peacock and the sparrow had more in common than you thought, ridiculous though the combination at first seemed? Life seemed to be full of such preposterous jokes—love's mansion, according to Yeats, pitched in the very place of excrement, romantic and idealistic love indebted not only to a strong philosophical tradition but also to the glands, man the naked ape yet also at times the glory, jest, and riddle of the world, joined finally in time to the timeless in the joke, the scandal, the wonder of the Incarnation. How many angels could dance on the head of a pin? How many peacocks could sit on a sparrow's back? It was perhaps all one thing and the same: peacock, sparrow, tears, laughter, life, death.

I remember my father crying "for joy" when my mother began recovering from a long illness, years later catching me to him in tears, to tell me how proud he was when I graduated from college. By the same token, I remember my own first words when I heard that a cousin was finally dead after years of debilitating, demeaning illness: "Thank God." These same words I was later to say when told of my own mother's death, after many years of suffering in both body and spirit, reflecting as I did so on her saying, so many years ago, that there were many things worse than death—an imponderable to a small boy but all too pertinent to adult wisdom.

I remember also laughing—to the scandal of one of the in-law aunts who always thought my father's family had a perverse sense of humor—at the horrific newspaper account of a woman over in Arkansas who drove up, in a rented car, to a family reunion, to which she had not been invited, and presented herself, dressed to the nines and also armed to the teeth, to the assembled family, five of whom she proceeded to shoot dead on the spot, hollering all the while for those who had escaped out the back door to

A Peacock on a Sparrow's Back

present themselves so she could shoot them also. A few days later, a similar instance occurred in Arizona: a man drove up, again in a rented car, to the house, where he mistakenly thought his wife was living with another man, and shot and killed them both. I tried explaining to my scandalized aunt that it wouldn't have been funny had the estranged woman, the incensed man secretly poisoned whole families: it was the boldness of their design, the flair of their quite literal executions that captured the humorous imagination—and the grisly comedy embodied in the idea that Hertz had indeed put them in the driver's seat or that Avis wasn't the only one who was trying harder. The advertisements were indeed coming true but in a way which probably not even Madison Avenue had envisioned. But how to explain the humor in such situations to people who thought things were exclusively good or bad, funny or sad, right or wrong?

The same principle really was embodied in a post-card message sent a friend of mine by an aunt of his who some years ago made a tour of Norway. And after inspecting the sights of Oslo and Bergen, with some assorted fjords and trolls thrown in for good measure, she wrote that they had made "a side trip to the Land of the Midnight Sun." I'm afraid my own aunt, as much as I love her, wouldn't have found that one funny either. I suppose people have to be very much at home in the world, though not necessarily worldly, to understand why such things are funny. Part of such laughter is laughter by default: one has to laugh to keep from crying. But there is also implied here a built-in belief that the world is somehow all one, big and little, that death and life aren't really so far apart, the grand and the trivial not so remote from each other, the universe not so apart from man that he can't fathom at least some portion of it. And one then laughs, maybe even from a form of sheer morning gladness, that the desert places are not so barren, either in the landscape or in the heart: the universe may be a monstrous joke played by purblind doomsters on puny little man; or maybe it's not even that but sheer hap, mere chance. Nevertheless, we laugh for joy that we can still see the joke, even if it's one played on us. That's man-

THE BURNING BUSH

hood, that's sanity, and perhaps it's one form of our salvation.

St. Paul observes that we are fools for Christ's sake, and it certainly takes a sort of foolishness to go along with the preposterous paradoxes propounded by the Good News, which, one figures, if he's got a grain of common sense, ought to be very bad news indeed. But it's not. And sometimes it's very human, even funny, even if in a heartbreaking way: all the disciples going to sleep on their Master in his bitter hour in the Garden, the braggart Peter vaunting his fidelity, only to be completely humbled by cock-crow, Martha's homely common-sense approach to washing the supper dishes (*somebody* has to be up and doing these things), only to be rebuked for being careful and troubled about such trivia, the Ethiopian eunuch going on his way rejoicing after his abrupt baptism, Jesus writing quietly in the sand (figuring? pondering?) before passing judgment on the woman taken in the very act of adultery. The list could be endless. And why shouldn't it be? One has got to be a sort of fool to believe in the Christian Gospel anyway: it's certainly imprudent at times—or seems so—not to be a child of this world rather than one of the children of light. And it's all put up to one on a very businesslike basis too: count the cost; sell all that you have and give it to the poor; be willing to leave mother, father, sister, and brother if need be. There are no punches pulled here, only plain talk and straight shooting. (The woman in Arkansas, the man in Arizona: they shot straight too. And I assume their talk was very plain indeed.)

This is all pretty far away from the childhood memories, the peacock sitting on the sparrow's back with which I started. But perhaps, in another way, it isn't far at all. It's only when we can comprehend that such absurd things can really be that we may be acquiring the beginnings of wisdom, along with the gift of laughter, the saving grace, and finally the spirit of truth.

O, What a One To Be Dead With!

Years ago now—when I was just a young girl—a man came through the country, taking everybody up in an airplane for five dollars a head. And I was simply dying to go and begged Mamma night and day until she finally gave in and let me. I'd seen all those old flying picture shows and read everything I could get my hands on about the Lafayette Escadrille and the Red Baron and his boys. And after all, I could remember when they were all more or less in business, in the headlines and all. So now you pretty much know how old I am, if you haven't already guessed it. Always look at a woman's hands, by the way: they generally tell the truth, even when her face and her hair don't.

Anyhow, I've seen everything—and ridden everything—now, from the open cockpit two-seater up to and including the Jumbo Jet. And I don't know but what we were just about as well off before: people all flying through the air now, getting wherever they're going so fast they meet themselves coming back and not knowing any more what to do or how and why to do it when they get there than they ever did before. And anyhow, it's not *travel*; it's just *transit*. And you go from A to B with nothing in between: you certainly don't see anything and there's not enough time to do anything along the way. So there you are, being shot through the air faster than cherubim and seraphim combined, probably; but your state of mind, to say nothing of your body, when you get there—assuming you do get there—is all pretty much neuter. There ain't no time for scenic views, to say nothing of shipboard romances, when you're going 600 miles an hour and seven miles high at that. At that rate, you're doing very well if you can manage to hold on to your false teeth and your wig and whatever other extras you're carrying. Flying don't do a thing for your mind or otherwise enlarge your horizons in any way that I can see.

Well, anyhow, it was a bit different back in the barnstorming

THE BURNING BUSH

days: everything had a more informal and certainly a less impersonal touch. And it was about as far as you can get from all the plastic food and music and service that you get on planes today. "Coffee, tea, or me?" indeed: you'd have to be pretty desperate to care, I should think. But I won't go into that now. If folks want to misbehave when they travel, they're going to do it, jet or no jet. Like Mamma said when that good-looking scoundrel, Arthur Hendren, left my cousin Sara and ran off with a chorus girl he met at the old Orpheum in Memphis: "Well, you see, he was a very attractive man; and he traveled a great deal and met other very attractive people." And then she would purse her lips and raise her eyebrows and look like she was on the point of winking but wouldn't. But then she never liked Sara either.

But the man that took me up for five dollars really looked the part, complete with helmet and goggles and the long white scarf. And I'm not sure but what he had a mustache too. Whatever the case, he was dreams come true and a gallant knight-crusader of the air, as far as I was concerned. Of course, I suspect he was probably as ugly as sin warmed over and his name was probably something impossible, like Sidebottom or Potts; but then that's history for you: it always gives you the facts and destroys the glamor. Or at least the wrong kind of glamor, which of course may not be a bad thing. But still you hate to let it go.

So along came Mr. Sidebottom or whatever his name was, and away we went, taking off from old Mrs. Murphy's cow pasture out on the edge of town that she had let him use for ten dollars as long as he was there. And I could have killed Mamma because, just before the gallant airman started revving up the propellers, she hollered, "Now don't you all go too fast or too far." And there I was about to be literally swept off the earth into what I hoped would be the land of heart's desire. And I'd paid five dollars for the privilege too, and there Mamma was trying to hold me down. I don't know to this very minute whether I've ever completely forgiven her for it either. Of course, as you get older, you learn that, in life, you do well not to go too fast or

O, What a One To Be Dead With!

too far, in lots of ways. But that's a hateful sort of knowledge, true as it may be—nothing but prudence, really, which can be a very tiresome virtue.

But what really deflated the whole balloon of my dreams or aspirations or whatever you want to call it was that, at the very last minute, who should priss up in her old Model T but Ada Belle Jordan, all dressed to kill and with her face painted within an inch of her life, and plonks down her five dollars and demands to be taken up as the other passenger. And three was going to be a crowd in that little plane, in more ways than one.

I don't know whether I'd been cherishing the very wildest dreams of high romance with Brother Sidebottom—all alone up in the wild blue yonder. But whatever I had been planning on was surely going to be changed by the advent of Ada Belle. She was a couple of years older than I was, and to say she was considered fast in those days would be to put it very mildly indeed. The Jordans were all of them a pretty sorry lot, and her mother being a Roberson didn't help any either. The girls in Ada Belle's family were all as wild as a buck as soon as they got out on the carpet, which, for them, was about the time they entered high school; and the boys all drank whiskey like it was so much water. But Ada Belle was about the limit.

Now how much she actually *did,* I don't know; in these days of the Pill and all the other prophylactics and permissives or whatever, we'd probably consider her about par for the course. What made Ada Belle different then, of course, was that she didn't seem to give a damn what anybody thought, and certainly she gave the *appearance* of being loose, which was all it took then. People don't seem to worry much about appearances these days, and sometimes I think it's a gain and sometimes I think it's a loss. I suppose it's still only a question of what it's the appearance *of,* which shows things in general haven't really changed much after all, though some of the particulars may have.

Anyhow, Ada Belle went "steady" with about five boys at one time, smoked in public, and was reported to have a very salty vocabulary. And her nickname around town—or at least among

THE BURNING BUSH

the younger set—was "Asbestos Pants," which all went back to the time she was practicing a fancy new dance step while waiting for a Coca-Cola at the soda fountain in Harris' Drug Store and old man Harris, who I always wondered how he got through high school, much less became a registered pharmacist (lazy as the Devil and not the brightest star in the firmament either), comes along and leers at Ada Belle and says, in the lewdest old way, out of the corner of his mouth, with all the juice from the tobacco he'd been chewing still trickling out, "If you don't watch out there, you're liable to drop something." And Ada Belle stops prancing just long enough to say, without batting an eye, "Well, it would be so hot an old man like you couldn't pick it up!" And I can tell you there was no more heard out of him that day, but Ada Belle passed into some kind of immortality in our town right on the spot.

From then on she was "Asbestos Pants," and I'm happy to say she went on from strength to strength in later life. I saw her on the streets of Memphis just the other day and hardly recognized her at all. She's on the third rich husband now and I suspect has had her face lifted. And God knows she's had her hair dyed—first henna, blonde now—often enough. But she's still going strong, and we had a good visit right there in the middle of Main Street and she told me all about her grandchildren and the trouble she'd had getting used to her new girdle.

But back in my flapper days, the last thing in the world I wanted was to be carried off in an airplane by my own private Lindbergh along with Asbestos Pants Jordan. And all I could think of at the moment we took off was us all being killed together in a very dramatic crash and the doleful tidings all spread out on the front page of next week's *Gazette;* and I thought, "O, what a one to be dead with!" Of course, now I wouldn't give a damn; but whether this represents a change in the times or in me (after all, I'm over forty years older now), I can't say. Perhaps it's both: most things usually are. And I suppose it was characteristic of a teen-ager to want to pick the company she wanted to be found dead with—shades of the *Titanic* and *Camille* and all

O, What a One To Be Dead With!

that sort of thing! Old people just naturally aren't so choosy.

On the other hand, we all do have our little rule-of-thumb judgments, you know. My husband always said the real test of a bar—whether it was a good place to be or just another convenience to get drunk in—was whether you would want to see all the people who were there at night—and in that dim religious light too, you wouldn't know your own grandpa—stone-cold sober, and in broad open daylight. And of course I really don't have much basis for judgment, being a woman my age and all; but I should think he was about correct. And God knows he'd had enough experience with bars to know. Maybe it's merely the difference between just drinking, which I've never really minded, and getting drunk, which I've always despised, heart, soul, and body. But I'd want to be as persnickety about choosing my company to be drunk with as who to be dead with, I can tell you.

On the other hand, like I said before, as you get older, some of these things seem to matter less and less: you're going to be dead anyhow, regardless of who with. And I can't think it'll make much difference to you one way or another. Like a very silly woman who told me once she was *never* really afraid to fly because she was always so well insured, to which I replied that, though her heirs might stand to profit from it, all that insurance wasn't going to do *her* much good. And she looked like all of a sudden she'd been told that her mother hadn't really been a D.A.R. and a pillar of the Presbyterian church all those years but instead had been the madam of a first-rate brothel, and I could begin to see *doubt* easing into her mind with all the subtlety of a brickbat, which, I assure you, would have been what it would have taken in her case.

Choosing who you're going to be dead with does seem of less importance as you get older: there's no doubt about that. Yet I don't think it's altogether an irrelevant consideration either. It's not the appearance of the thing that matters so much but the idea: you won't be there to see it yourself but you can imagine what it would be like for the ones that are left behind to tell the tale. Like one of the Morrises—that crowd out at Louisa—that

THE BURNING BUSH

died that time in a room down at the Peabody Hotel in Memphis, in the company of "a lady other than his wife." And the paper went on to say the doctor gave the cause of his death as a heart attack, brought on by "excitement." Well, I don't reckon you'd want to be dead that way, if only for your family's sake. But I for one wished old Paul Morris well and was glad he made such a splendid exit. Not many folks die from excitement; most of them have had little enough of it in their lives. On the whole, I guess that, as you get older, you'd better worry not so much about *who* you're going to be dead with as *what* you're going to be dead with. And I think that's most people's problem, if they only knew it, in life as well as in death.

Honk If You Love Jesus

Well, you just never know what you're going to run into when you drive down the highway in this part of the world. Why, the other day, I was headed down toward Memphis on the old highway we don't use much now that the interstate has come in; but that was because I was going to see Ann Louise—that's my younger sister that married that off-brand Holy Roller preacher that had a church that *sounded* like it was called "the Savior's Tabernacle" or "a Nazarene passed by" or some such carrying on or maybe it was "Pentecostal Holiness" or something like that. Anyhow, Ann Louise's husband's church is way out there in the thickets of the Loosahatchie Bottom this side of Memphis, and you feel like you're going into the darkest interior of the African jungles every time you turn off the old road and head back to the place they live—called Frog Jump, if you can believe something so ridiculous.

Anyhow, what to my wondering eye should appear but a brand-new billboard all rigged up beside the old highway right of way, and it showed a clock with the hands pointing to five minutes before noon or midnight (midnight, I guess, since it was all on a black background). And down at the bottom, in big bold letters—black of course, it said: "Time is running out. Where will *you* spend eternity?" And then it invited you to attend the nearest church of your choice—provided of course it was a Baptist church. Really, I used to think you could make some sort of interesting list of all the Baptist churches just between here and Memphis: sometimes two or three in the same neighborhood, to judge by the signs pointing off the main road at the same turn-off, and all of them with names like "Maranatha" or "Bethesda" or "Shiloh" or something else equally uncompromising. Of course I'm not sure what the list would have *meant* except that the woods are fuller of Baptists around here than weevils in a flour barrel. Maybe they're all in competition with each other, as well as with

THE BURNING BUSH

the Devil. I always thought I'd figure it out sometime when I had some extra time on my hands.

But anyhow there was this big sign blaring at you right there in your face; and I reckoned it was all supposed to "make you stop and think," like they say. But it all left me pretty cold, because I used to live—when my husband was alive—up in the mountains of East Tennessee, where it wasn't anything to see "Jesus Is Coming" or "Prepare To Meet Thy God," all written over the side of some mountain on one of those God-awful hairpin turns that had already scared the filling out of you anyway. And I always thought the Lord or the Devil or whoever was in charge of the signs would have pretty slim pickings after that.

But anyhow I hadn't expected to see such monstrosities all spread out over West Tennessee, which I always have thought was the least tacky part of the state, if nothing else. Of course, that would mortify everybody in Nashville to death—think they're the seat of culture and "the Athens of the South" and more churches there than fleas on a coon dog and so forth (East Tennessee I've already written off as a lost cause, you'll notice). But really, you don't have to dig very deep in Middle Tennessee, Nashville included, to see that old red clay dirt beneath the surface. They may have put rhinestones on the cowboys on Grand Ole Opry and deodorized the hog lot out of them, but they sure God ain't been able to do that for the audience, I can tell you. And don't tell me they cry all the way to the bank, either. Some people are just *born* tacky and that's that: it all sort of makes a Presbyterian out of you.

And of course I always have thought that Middle Tennessee outfit gave themselves far too many airs about the Confederacy and their "Southern heritage" and so forth. If truth was told, I don't imagine many of them were very far ahead of being Union sympathizers then *and* now: the "pivot" in the state, I believe they like to call themselves. Well, I've never known a "pivot" yet that could let their word be yea, yea or nay, nay. What they really want is to have it both ways and not pay any of the bills: a border state really, and you know better than to expect any-

Honk If You Love Jesus

thing out of *them*. Same mentality as Atlanta, really, where everybody in East Tennessee always thought they would go when they died if they'd been good: do anything in the world for a dollar and give their soul to be a little New York, I always thought, General Sherman or no.

Well, anyhow, here was this redneck mentality blazoned forth on the highway; and it practically gave me the pip to see it. The next thing we knew, there was liable to be a Baptist missionary or something hiding behind every tree. We've just barely voted in package stores, as it is; and that might set progress back another generation. Understand now: I'm a Methodist born and bred and happy in my persuasion, though I've thought it wouldn't hurt a bit to put a few mourners' benches back in the church these days. Mighty far from John Wesley now, if you ask me. But then I should talk because there was Ann Louise—my own sister—that married this ungodly Church of God or Nazarene or whatever he was preacher that she never in this world would have looked at twice if Mamma hadn't strictly forbidden her to set eyes on him that summer he spent here in town doing "mission work" when he was going to Bible college or whatever they call it. I doubt they ever heard of a theological school, much less a seminary.

Of course, it could have been worse; and he could have been a hard-shell Baptist, where you don't need any special training for the ministry because the Lord just puts the words in your mouth, like they say. Or she could have married a Mormon and had the pleasure of doing without coffee and tea, to say nothing of alcohol and tobacco, for the rest of her natural life and maybe even gotten into more peculiar situations than that, like the woman Mamma met over at Hot Springs one time when she went to take the baths for her rheumatism that had turned into a Mormon late in life and then married her own husband all over again, after he had been dead for twenty years. Or old Mrs. Pringle down the street from us that got senile when she was over ninety and began to worry about the validity of her baptism because she was born a Methodist but had married Mr. Pringle,

THE BURNING BUSH

who was a Baptist when he worked at it, which wasn't very often really. But anyhow they—her children, that is—had a time with her till they got the Methodist preacher to come tell her the Lord wasn't running any waterworks: He was just concerned about the sign and the symbol, so to speak.

Well, I reckon Ann Louise could have done worse, along the lines I've stated just now. But Otis—that's her husband of course—hadn't been too long out of the backwoods—back water too, for that matter—when she caught him; and she's had to devote most of her time, really, to making him fit for public consumption, to say nothing of public viewing. Big gawky rawboned fellow, red hair and all. With a name like "Otis" and a background like his (father named Lee Roy, mother named Hortense), I'm sure you've got a pretty good idea of what he looks like. And, on the whole, I'd say she'd been able to raise Otis up a good deal, which I think the woman usually has it in her power to do if she wants to. Double standard, I know, but I'm old-fashioned and too old to change now. And they've got two well behaved children, though the boy *is* talking about going to Bible college when he gets older (or maybe it's a school for evangelistic song leaders—I forget) and the girl can't make up her mind whether cosmetics may all be just vanity. Well, for some people they are, and that's all there is to it: what *they* need is for God Almighty to just start all over with them—and from the nub. On the other hand, I don't see anything wrong with using the sense God gave you and improving on nature if there's room for it, which, with most of us, there certainly is.

And Ann Louise is forty-five next July, and I'm five years older, and I reckon we both look it. But we're still here and turned loose on the public, and that's more than some folks can say. And, gradually, you know, I think she's been putting a good shellac on Otis so he won't embarrass her to death socially; and she's gotten him so he can move his bowels without seeing the hand of God in it and practically everything else he does and says. Now you understand, I'm not knocking the fundamentalist folks as such: I think a right good strong dose of shouting might

Honk If You Love Jesus

improve the health of the Methodist Church right here in town enormously. And God only knows what it would do for the Presbyterians, to say nothing of the Episcopalians. On the other hand, I'd just as soon folks not have Jesus so much on the brain or in the mouth. Because then I'm always perverse enough to think, well, maybe that's because they haven't got Him anywhere else, if you see what I mean.

Well, anyhow, all this was more or less running around in my mind when I was driving down to Ann Louise's last week, to spend the day, and especially after I up and saw that damned sign with the five-minutes-to-go clock (just like it was a football game or something). And it made me mad all over again because I thought that was just what was wrong in the South, maybe all over the country now: too much Jesus in public and not enough in private. (And I don't much care whether you're talking about Jesus freaks or Oral Roberts, the bearded or the bare.) But what really got my goat was when I drove up in Ann Louise's driveway, and there was their station wagon (they really should have a tank for negotiating some of the terrain Otis has to slog back into to feed his sheep, as you may say) with a bumper sticker on it saying, "Honk If You Love Jesus."

Now of course it might have been worse: it could have said "See Rock City" or "Stop at Stuckey's." But with the kind of mind I've got, to say nothing of the opinions I hold, you can just imagine what all I was able to dream up in the way of dramatic moments, with that sign for a starter: expressways full of loving, honking Christians or highways full of silent agnostics or maybe even atheists ringing cow bells or sounding a siren (which I still want to call "sireen," though Mamma never would let me because she said it sounded niggerish) to show they *hated* Jesus, for all I knew. I guess what really gave me the willies, though, was the idea of just *honking* over Jesus, like He was just another Howard Johnson's or Holiday Inn, or else a reminder to drive carefully on the Fourth of July. Whatever else you could do with Jesus (and I wasn't sure you could *do* anything with Him), I was pretty sure you couldn't just *honk* about Him. (And I'm no

THE BURNING BUSH

religious fanatic either.) But bow your head, cross yourself even (mercy, what would Mamma say to that, that was heard to remark, when they were building the first Catholic Church ever in captivity here, that nobody was doing a *thing* about it?); but honk, no. *That* I did have pretty strong feelings about and intended to make myself known to Ann Louise if not to Otis himself.

All right, so maybe it was just a sign between Christians, like some Masonic falderal or some foolishness in a college fraternity, and they were all members of a secret society and had to stick together in these dark days. I could go along with that, I reckoned. I guess it was just the honking that I didn't like: you just didn't acknowledge Jesus that way. Maybe by the screams of martyrs or the silent sufferings of saints, to say nothing of the joyful shouts of the everyday garden variety of redeemed sinners; but no, not with a toot—and a passing toot at that. Whatever else He was, Jesus Christ was neither a hitchhiker nor a filling station attendant. When the right time came along, I could see I was going to have to speak to Ann Louise and Otis about that.

Show the Gentleman What You Have

I grew up in the small-town South during the Thirties; and I think there were only three Jewish families in our town, and probably not more than five in our county. And I knew that people made jokes about them in those difficult times. (Question: "What's the fastest thing on two wheels?" Answer: "A Jew on a bicycle getting out of Germany.") But then, presumably, they always had; and the Bible explained why: "He came unto his own, and his own received him not." And that was supposedly the reason they had had such a difficult time all these many years, at least under the Christian dispensation. On the other hand, my father always said he didn't have anything for or against them one way or the other; but, if you had eyes in your head, you could just see who was making the most money out of Christmas, without even believing in Jesus Christ. He was a hardware merchant, and I've often wondered what he would have said if he'd been in the dry-goods business.

But that was always the way with him: holding something up and turning it round and seeing both sides or more to the case until you just wished he would just go on and come to the lick-log and fish or cut bait: like the Bible, say yea, yea or nay, nay. But he didn't really have any ill will towards Jews, and he said you could just take note of what had happened to every nation or leader that had ever tried to give them trouble: they all, sooner or later, had had to eat crow and take backwater. "The Bible says they're the Lord's chosen people: if you know what's good for you, you better let them alone." And that was his considered opinion on the matter and probably wasn't subject to any change, at least not in the present era. Most of his opinions were like that.

My mother certainly didn't have anything much one way or the other about Jews on her mind either. One of her friends, Mrs. Sternberger, belonged to her bridge club, though I don't think they socialized much in any other situation. But then the Thurs-

THE BURNING BUSH

day Bridge Club was situation enough for most anybody: none of your desserts or Coke parties like they have now, but a regular full-length luncheon (I got to lick the dasher for the apricot ice cream when Mamma entertained them) for the "girls," as they always called themselves. And believe you me, they dressed up for the event, too. God knows what they would have thought of pants suits and "casual" clothes. No gloves of course (*that* was for the Book Club), but pretty much everything else. And they played for *blood*.

Anyhow, Miriam Sternberger belonged to the Thursday Bridge Club; but Mamma said it didn't disrupt anything because she wasn't *orthodox* (a very mysterious and somehow terrifying word to me) and so could eat country ham whenever you had that. (What fool wouldn't, I wondered.) So I knew Jews had funny ideas about their food; and then later on when one of my closest friends in high school was Sam Goldstein, I learned about meat dishes and milk dishes and not mixing them together and so on. And they weren't supposed to eat shrimp or lobster, which was certainly no problem in the West Tennessee of those days, anyhow. In fact, Sam said it mostly all had to do with what was or was not hygienic in the Israel of Old Testament days and really made sound nutrition sense then, if you just thought about it.

So I grew up, knowing the Sternbergers and the Goldsteins. (Another Jewish family, the Levys, didn't rank so well, even with their own people, though I never knew why: Daddy said it probably all had something to do with them sending their children up North to school and being too free and easy with the Negroes.) And really, I never thought much about any of them *as Jews*. I suppose a sociologist now would say they were thoroughly acculturated or something, which sounds like making buttermilk or yogurt. And they were, most of them, apparently Southern in their opinions or, as the same sociologists would probably say, their prejudices. They were mainly just people who didn't go to church with us, though they would always come when there was a special Youth Rally or something like that— more a community thing than a religious exercise. But there

Show the Gentleman What You Have

weren't even enough of them to have a synagogue or whatever at home or even a cemetery of their own, so they had to go to Memphis to worship and be buried and so on.

I guess the real parting of the ways, for most of us—us and them too—came when we all went off to college. And they joined their fraternities and we joined ours, and they started going with their girls and we with ours. I know one time one of the Sternberger girls was going pretty strong with one of the Williamson boys at home, but they were still in high school, so nobody took much notice of it. I don't think, for a minute, either of them thought it might come to something. Their parents, as far as I know, didn't even *worry* about it: nothing serious could possibly happen.

Well, that shows how far we've come these days, I suppose, whether for good or ill. If they're going steady now—white, black, Jew, Gentile, or whatever—you automatically assume they're going steady in *every* way. And you have to decide whether you want them to get married and whether it might not be a good thing anyhow: at least you don't have "outside" babies that way for grandchildren. Now of course, it looks as though we're about to have "abortion on demand"—maybe like Dr. Spock's "feeding on demand." And, for all *I* know, there may be some connection between the two; but I tell my two—and my wife does too—we'd just as lief be notified of their intentions first, whether it's marriage, abortion, or whatever. Change, yes: God knows, we've got plenty of that. Sometimes more than we can consume on the premises. Progress? I'm not so sure, because of course that assumes you're moving toward something desirable—or you take it to be such. And I haven't made up my mind about our case yet, not by a long shot.

Well, as I was saying, the thought of such a mixed relationship, to say nothing of marriage, simply wasn't entertained in my time. And as things in Europe began getting rougher for the Jews and I began noticing more and more pictures in *Life* magazine (which is where I tell my children I learned the facts of *life*—no pun intended—in most every way: not a bad way either, though it

THE BURNING BUSH

still puts me off the Germans and the Japanese), I began, for the first time, to really *think* about the Jews, which I never had really before. Of course, if you have only two or three families of them on hand, you don't have a problem, anyhow. But there were the Sternberger family and my friend, Sam Goldstein; and, though I knew there were ugly jokes about Jews (tight-fisted, schemers, shirkers of manual labor, all that sort of thing), I never really thought of those things applying to any of my friends. They were just that: friends. And I didn't see why their being of another group had anything to do with their being mistreated.

Certainly, I thought anybody that touched a hair of Miriam Sternberger's head would have had to answer to the Thursday Bridge Club for it. And though I used to tease Sam about being the potential Messiah, to say nothing of the jokes we used to make about being or not being circumcised, I knew I felt the same way about him. I wasn't sure how formidable I might seem as a foe of "racial prejudice," as it was now called. But if I had been Hitler, I would have thought twice before tangling with the Thursday Bridge Club. But then I thought that might have been part of his trouble anyhow: he hadn't had enough lady dragons to do business with, only fairly tame Valkyries. It would have made a different man out of him: better, I don't know, but different, yes. (That sounds like an affectation of Yiddish phraseology, doesn't it; and I didn't really intend that either. Do you suppose I got that from television?)

So we never had any outbursts, good or bad, in my town, when I was growing up—not about Jews, at any rate. But the more they got persecuted in Europe (and I think I thought or worried about it more than the Sternbergers or the Goldsteins), the more fascinating they became to me. How were they so different from us? Some differences were obvious; they were often dark-complexioned, with different facial bone structures sometimes. Eating different food and observing different holidays, yes. But still, did they think or feel different on the inside of themselves? Of course, no one joked about the more obvious differences more

Show the Gentleman What You Have

than they did themselves, like Miriam Sternberger telling about the time she was hiring a new cook—colored of course. And just as a matter of course, she asked her whether she had ever worked for any Jews before; and the colored woman said, "No'm, but I done worked for white folks." And the Thursday Bridge Club thought that was hilarious. But did Miriam think it was really so funny as she seemed to—or was she telling it as "protective coloration," like I was learning about in biology? Maybe in those days—the war years—they felt they had to do that. But again, none of that foolishness—Hitler, purges, pogroms, or whatever—even remotely percolated down into Tennessee; and, besides, when you have so few of them, who needs a holy war? The Negro situation—or what we could see shaping up as a situation—was enough to occupy most people's minds, if you were thinking about that sort of thing.

I think I just felt more and more uneasy about it—and not, you understand, that I was about to embark on a "flaming liberal" young-adult kick either. The Jews were just *there*; they just sat there and had been doing so for, lo, these many thousands of years. Maybe that's what people really couldn't forgive them for. You stomped on them, you killed them off, you carted them off to the gas ovens or whatever other atrocity you had in mind; but they always rose up again somewhere else. Like Johnson grass or the seven-year itch or having the wolf by the ears. You had them, and they had you. And you couldn't get rid of them, like apparently you could lots of other people and nations. Whether the Lord still had hold of them and wouldn't let them go or whether it was the other way around and they wouldn't let Him go—it really didn't matter. Somehow, they stayed, whether you liked it or not. Of course, later on, after I went off to college up East, I learned more about the ins and outs of Jewry and Judaism and why some of them I would have given my life for and others I'd have lit the first match to—exasperating, infuriating, yet endearing as they could be. (I finally decided it was the secularized, deracinated ones I detested the most: when you've had a God like Jehovah working on you, you don't turn your back on Him with

THE BURNING BUSH

impunity. Or that's the way it seemed to me.) But anyhow, the main thing was that the Jews stayed: they wouldn't be killed off or ignored out of existence. Again, they just always *were*.

And that brings me to an anecdote my father used to love to tell about one of the old Jewish merchants of our town—long since in Abraham's bosom, where I hope he's resting comfortably. And his name was Mr. Popkin, and he had a wife named Bertha. And one day somebody—a man—from out at Haley's Switch or some other wild prospect in the tall and uncut came in and asked to see some low-priced men's underwear that Mr. Popkin had advertised as being on sale. And so Mr. Popkin didn't do a thing but turn round to his wife, who wasn't any taller than five feet if that, and command her: "Bertha, now get up on top of that counter and pull down your drawers and show the gentleman what you have for fifty cents." And as Daddy approached the punch line, he would begin waving his customary big cigar around, as though conducting an orchestra, which, in many ways, he was every time he talked—ordering, marshaling, shaping, forming his words and sentences for maximum effectiveness and thereby bringing into being a harmonious whole. And when he came to "show the gentleman what you have for fifty cents," he would flourish the cigar about raffishly yet triumphantly, to show that he was finishing off the story in good form—substance, timing, and all. And he was well pleased with his handiwork, as indeed he had good reason to be. My mother always pretended to be mildly scandalized with this story, but I loved it. And the more I thought about it, the better I liked it. I knew of course it wouldn't do to tell when I was at school up East: they wouldn't have understood at all and would have assumed I was wrapped up in "Southern bigotry" or whatever. Geography has a lot to do with what people think is funny, you know—sad but true, I've found.

But the last time I was home—I live in Memphis now—I saw Sam Goldstein for the first time in a good many years. We hadn't drifted apart except in the most intangible and inevitable of ways: he married one woman and stayed home, minding the store, quite

Show the Gentleman What You Have

literally, whereas I married another one and went off to seek my fortune in the Big City. And all of a sudden, it occurred to me (I still don't know why: was I testing something—myself, Sam, both of us, what?) to tell Sam my father's old story about Mr. Popkin; so I plunged in without really wondering whether Sam would like it or perhaps even take offense. But as I approached the punch line, I grew apprehensive: how did I know Sam was the same as he was when we were in high school together? Would he laugh, would he turn on his heel and walk off, or what? I would have given a great deal, at that point, never to have embarked on the tale of Mr. Popkin and Bertha and the fifty-cent drawers. But I was in too far to back out now, so I had to continue. But when I got to the punch line, I'm afraid I showed my embarrassment pretty plainly: I lowered my voice and didn't even look at Sam. But, God bless him, he threw back his head and laughed, just like in the old days. And then, as though he might have sensed how I felt, he gripped my arm and said, "Listen, Buster, don't you know that's why us Jews are still here, after all these years? We're still showing folks what we have, and it's still a quality product, but we've done gone up on the price. Fifty cents wouldn't even buy you a jock-strap now! And people don't appreciate anything they get for nothing. You ought to know us better than that by now." "Yes," I replied, as I slapped him on the back; and it was just like old times. "I suppose I should."

What Papa Said

or

Sleeping Under Two Blankets Every Night

When I was growing up, everybody I knew in my hometown went off somewhere in the summer except us. But my father said vacations were all foolishness, he had never had one in his life, and, besides, he needed to stay there and look after his store. And it was money we didn't need to spend: I ought to think about my education, which was what we should be saving for. Anyhow, why did anybody want to travel? Memphis was about as far as he ever wanted to get from home, and not very often at that. (And he had *been* to New York, back before the First World War.)

But that was how I got to see all the new movies (I called them picture shows) before they came to the Dixie Theater at home: Daddy would have to run down to Memphis to one of the wholesalers some hot summer afternoon, and I would get to spend a couple of hours at Loew's State, where it really was twenty degrees cooler inside, like the advertisements said. But what was the point of air conditioning if you didn't feel the cold? Daddy said he remembered the first electric fan he ever saw, though; and he wouldn't swap it for one of these newfangled attic fans that everybody was always bragging on how well you could cool the whole house by, especially at night. But he wouldn't give you fifty cents for one of them, he said: they didn't even blow on you so you could *tell* you were getting cooler. And the day of houses with their own automatic air conditioning was just not something he cared to even think about.

But anyhow, everybody we knew was always going off to the Smoky Mountains or the Gulf of Mexico or *somewhere* in the summer and sending us back post cards that said they were fine

THE BURNING BUSH

and hoped we were too and they were all sleeping under two blankets every night. And I hated and despised them all in my heart because I had never seen a mountain or the ocean and there we were almost on the Mississippi River and running the electric fans night and day but still burning up alive and getting eaten up by mosquitoes and not going anywhere or doing anything and not expecting any change either. I even had malaria a couple of times, and that's the worst thing I know that you can have, not to kill you. But the mountains and the oceans remained—and still do—for me wonderful symbols of travel and trips and vacations and all sorts of glamorous things. And it used to worry me that my father never wanted to see them and was so well content to stay at home with his own folks, like he said. I even thought he was proud of not traveling, as though there were some sort of inherent virtue in just standing still or just taking a seat in the same place all the time. And maybe my own desire to travel and see the mountains and the ocean and the great cities and sleep under two blankets every night was some sort of reaction against that.

Anyhow, after I went off to college, I did do some traveling; and I loved it as much as I ever thought I would. I didn't know whether it was broadening me like people always said it would, but at least I thought I knew the folks back home better than ever. And that was some sort of gain, because then you had something else to compare them with. And that was a something that didn't give a hoot in Hell about who Grandpa was or whether he was bank president or Sunday School superintendent for forty years or whether Grandma's father gave her $10,000 to build a new house with when she married, which was practically the riches of Croesus in those days. But the main thing they couldn't have cared less about was what Papa said.

And that all has to do with the brand of folks that I'd put on the same level with the ones that had to go off and write back they were sleeping under two blankets every night. Because that was the one story of their whole lives and the only thing, really, that gave them importance or consequence—who Papa was and how much money he'd made and how respected he was in the community and so on and so forth until death did you part. Sometimes it was "Father" or "Pa" or "Papa," but it didn't make any difference, and the rose smelled the same by whatever name it was called. And there never had been anybody in the whole wide world like Papa, for rectitude, probity, wisdom, prudence, piety, and, always, prosperity.

So it was two classes of people that I hated: the travelers and the backgrounders. And I realize now we'd call their respective ploys some form of gamesmanship, along with the strategy of nothing ever being as good as it used to be and food not tasting the same and no real quality anywhere anymore. They were all deriving their significance from something that had nothing to do with whether they themselves had any sense or any ability. In a way, of course, the groups were dissimilar: the what-Papa-saiders weren't much on travel because, after all, when you got somewhere else, the people there had never heard of Papa and didn't care what he'd said when or where. And so their occupation was gone. Come to think of it, maybe the two-blanket-sleepers were their complements because that was all they did have in their lives—what no Papa never did not say nowhere. *They* were making it on their own—justification not by the works of others but theirs.

But neither one of these groups really knew where they were or you or me either because they couldn't put the at home and the far off really together. They didn't know that you really take home with you wherever you go, that it shapes and defines your perception of other places, that you inevitably see the foreign through the eyes of home but, when you return home, your views on it have been modified by what you've seen afar or abroad. And you can't really know the one without the other. But, in so doing, you go beyond the sleeping under two blankets and you get out of the range of what Papa said. You achieve your own identity then in a way you never could have before: you know where you are because you know where you came from originally, where you've been to since, and where you've returned to now.

The what-Papa-saiders are in complete command of the home

THE BURNING BUSH

terrain, just as the two-blanket-sleepers ride the whirlwind and direct the storm of sheer movement. But neither one knows where he's really at because he has no other spectacles to look at it all through. And they all keep repeating themselves, in one way or another, wherever you go. The what-Papa-saiders, if they can ever be persuaded to travel, find that nothing they eat ever agrees with them and the hotels are never clean (my own father said you could always tell that people who complained unduly about the food they ate "out" had all been raised on branch water, which is perfectly true, so maybe Papa wasn't such a fine gentleman after all); and the two-blanket-sleepers will always find out where you haven't been and then tell you that's the very place you should have gone first of all. And of course the food wherever you are now used to be good but it's not anymore, now that things are not normal, which you know they never were in the first place. Usually, when things were normal, Papa was alive, had plenty of money, and was going to take care of *you*; that's what most people believe by the term. Whatever was normal was what you didn't have to worry about.

I've spent a good deal of my life, one way or another, trying to get away from these two sets of folks, maybe even be revenged on them for what they did to my childhood and adolescence. Why? They would have taught me to despise the really admirable qualities in my home and the life there because they never, never could match up to the far off, whether in time or in space. And that's really what both these groups are: romantics, nonrealists of a sort. Because it's always either what you never knew, whether in space or in time, that is superior to what you have known, what you know now, where you've been, where you are now— your own self, your own home. And I think that's unforgivable. Perhaps I shouldn't speak of them so bitterly had they not come so close to working their will on me: there was a time when I did think I despised my own time, my own place because it wasn't what Papa said or didn't have two blankets on the bed every night. But I think I did find out, after a while, that neither view was exclusively valid, that, in a sense, they complemented each other and a really sensible view of life at home and elsewhere had to comprehend, finally transcend them both. Another way of putting it would be to say that history and geography should always go together. You really can't know one without the other. And only when you know them both can you be freed of the tyranny each is capable of exercising alone. Only then can you know yourself and finally possess yourself. In the end, making a lifework out of what Papa said forty years ago and sleeping under two blankets every night is really nothing but two different forms of slavery.

I've Been Dying All My Life; How About You?

Our house was right on the street to the cemetery; and every time there was a big funeral, my nurse and I would sit out on the front steps and watch the procession go by, noticing what sort of flowers there were on the casket and how many cars made up the group and which ones the family were in and all that sort of thing. And to this day, you know, there are a lot of people in my hometown whom I have no recollection of as living persons; but I well remember their funerals. And I don't know that that's necessarily very morbid either. Children are naturally impressed with the dramatic and ceremonial, and that they should remember such things should come as no surprise. But, Good Lord, I remember the weddings too! It wasn't all dying, you know.

And of course all of us crave drama, to some extent, to help us make sense out of life, which often seems meaningless and aimless enough. I didn't realize it at the time but I do now: that was why I felt the way I did when one of my cousins—a very much loved one—was killed overseas during the Second World War. We weren't even notified till after he had been dead a month, and then were given the details of how he died, where he was buried, and so on. But it was all presented as a *fait accompli,* and so our grief just went on and on—with nothing like a funeral to wind it up or settle it. I suppose anthropologists would say we all find rites of passage necessary as we go through life, but I think I could make it simpler by just saying we all need to have some order—even a spurious one—imposed on the most shattering moments in life—so that we can bear them and keep on living after they have happened, or at least know what has happened to us, whether of joy or sorrow. And you can call it whatever you like—our attempts to make sense out of all such shocks and alarms. Whatever makes you happy, I say; but we *have* got to

THE BURNING BUSH

have them—the ceremonies, the rituals, the dramatic moments.

But this is all beside the point because what I really wanted to talk to you about here was death and how I came to know about it and feel about it and why it has been on my mind more or less all my life. I grew up, of course, around older people: my parents were old enough to have been my grandparents, and to this day I suppose I'm more at home with the geriatric set than with either youth or maturity. And always, always there was somebody in the family or somebody down the street dying off in our little town. And you can't do anything privately in a place like that, remember. Death is no secret, and your friends not only help you prepare for it—when it's someone you love—but help you with the aftermath, whether it's with covered dishes, flowers, kind words, or a silent pressure of the hand. They help you get ready for the onset, the advent of the Great Fact, then help you make your life over afterwards.

But why did people die—and not always just the old ones either? When I would ask my nurse, she would just look mysterious and say, "Well, their time had just done come." But what did that mean? My mother's explanation was no better either: "Mrs. So-and-so died because she just couldn't get well." But what was the rhyme, the reason to the whole thing? I didn't know then, and I'm not really any wiser now. But death as a fact, death as a reality was very early present in my life; and no one in our family ever tried to gloss it over either. None of us ever "passed away." We died, period. And we got buried in a grave in a cemetery, and nobody tried to pretend we were not going to go back to earth, ashes to ashes, dust to dust. And I suppose it was all very salutary in some ways: that idea, held long enough in your mind, was bound to keep you from getting too big for your breeches. All around you was death—among those you loved, among those you didn't even know, among all nations on the face of the earth, and the very earth and the Creation itself. It was all, in one way or another, dying. And you had to come to terms with that great central fact of life. It was no good pretending it didn't exist or trying to cover it up with euphemisms: that would

I've Been Dying All My Life

have been treating it like an anomaly or even an obscenity. Very often my father would preface his most emphatic remarks with, "Now you know, just as surely as you know you're born to die. . . ." And many another speaker would echo him. For them it was all perfectly natural, in every sense.

But I sometimes wonder: did I get too big an overdose of death somewhere along the line? Did I not see it as more than the great central fact of life, even the definer of life, which of course it is? Did I not perhaps make too big a thing of it somehow, somewhere? After all, life is for the living and it has to be lived. And the dead should be left alone to bury their dead. Yet again, what do you do with your ghosts? We all have them: people we've loved, people we've hated, memories that won't stay dead and buried but, for good or for ill, do walk abroad, sometimes to bless but, quite often, seeking whom they may devour. As the old saw has it: memories that bless and burn. And indeed they do, and I should think we ignored them at our peril. You can't cut yourself off from the past, any more than you can the present: if you could, I should say it was a very unhealthy thing to do. You'd be headed round the bend for sure. Because the ghosts must be dealt with: they can't just be sent about their business. And they are just as real as death—and life—itself.

Again, where did I go wrong, if I did? I'm not sure; but I think it was in believing that, since one had to die eventually, he might as well go on and get it over with—the fear and trembling, the sickness unto death, which come with thoughts of that last bitter hour. And what must be at last had, in one way or other, better be soon. But that's wrong too because it discounts life, the glory of the present day, the radiance of this particular dawn, the sunshine of this very noon bearing down upon you like the very valid fact which it is too, before declining into the lengthening shadows of afternoon and evening. They're all real too—and as real as death. And you never really prepare for death, you know; and I'm not talking about a necessarily religious question now. After all, which of us can comprehend our not being here, really and truly returning to earth, as some part of an endless cycle which

THE BURNING BUSH

repeats itself on into perpetuity—or as far as makes it seem so to us? To imagine, to figure to ourselves, as the French say, our own deaths is, for most of us, an impossibility. And yet, with the thinking part of our minds, we all know that yes, we are going to die, really and truly, and the world will go right on without us, and it will more or less be as if we had never lived. Insulting, maddening, but true.

Where I think my own death-knowledge and death-thoughts got out of hand was in my thinking they rendered life an irrelevant matter, something to be ignored as a temporary affair, with thoughts then firmly fixed beyond time in eternity, whether in a religious context or something else. (But then couldn't the present be part of eternity too?) Was it all a sort of Byzantine maneuver—like the flat icons which seem to ignore the depth of the flesh, the third dimension of the right here, the right now? I've often wondered. Of course, one can't ignore the religious dimension either, which in my case was Southern evangelical: no Holy Rollers in my background but the Day of Pentecost was in the air. The times were hastening on too, so the flesh was perhaps not so much a present evil as a mere impertinence. Of course, my theology isn't so far-fetched as it may sound here: the Eastern Church, I believe, has always made the Third Person of the Trinity more important than we have in the West, and it's been suggested that Southern Protestantism is a religion of the Holy Ghost. And I think that's a very valid observation.

Certainly, it was exaggerated out of relation to the Incarnation, even at times perhaps the Creator-Father Himself. The Dove descending seemed somehow more immediate, I believe; after all, the Creation was a fact but was wearing out, running down. The Atonement was real, yes; but was the Son a man of flesh just like ourselves? Could you really believe that? If you could, so many things became easier, the Good News itself even better. But this was only at times because always there seemed to be the Holy Ghost brooding over my world, as on the first day of Creation itself. And the sin against Him was the one that would not be forgiven, either in this world or the next. How awful, how

I've Been Dying All My Life

unspeakable, and yet how deliciously terrifying! Something so final, so never-never that imagination could simply not comprehend it—any more, really, than it could infinity.

Well, I hadn't intended to go off on this long theological tangent; but, Doctor, Father (whatever you want me to call you), you asked me what I thought had been the principal reasons why I felt like I did about death. Somewhere I know it all went wrong. I've been telling you the way I know I perhaps ought to feel about it; but more and more I've been seeing myself drowning into death—myself and all the Universe, filling up with death, a dying system strangling in its own filth, its own exhaust fumes, running down as it runs out of gas, and headed for sure oblivion. And I know that's true, and you know it's true. But tell me why I'm so obsessed with the idea. Is it that I'm afraid of life, the risk it involves always, whether with people or with things? Death, after all, can be managed when you're the one left alive to tell the tale. But life—and the living—can all change so quickly. And it can all be so hard to manage. Death often seems so much easier even if it scares you silly: no more stress, no more thought, no more decisions. Anyhow, tell me what you think, please, because I've reached a time in my life—I've just turned forty, you know—where it's all about to drive me crazy. It's not a game any more now; I realize that. Sooner or later, really and truly, it *is* going to happen to me.

What Do You Want To Have Written on Your Tombstone?

I remember how put out my mother was one time when a woman she was supposed to call about being at the church to help when the Missionary Society was going to serve the monthly dinner for the Board of Stewards (and now you'll know right off it was the *Methodist* Church I'm talking about) told her she couldn't possibly come because her baby was so sick. In fact, she had sat up all night the night before, she said, trying to decide what she was going to have written on his tombstone. And Mamma didn't think much of that, whether it was in jest or in earnest. She said she thought Mrs. Evans, which was the lady's name, would have done a lot better to see about getting her baby well and let the tombstone business take care of itself, which of course it would. But then Mamma was always like that—practical; and I don't imagine she ever sat down in her life many times just to have a good cry over something. What would have been the *use* of it all, she would have asked you. Still, a lot of people would agree that there are lots of times when you do have to sit down and cry—whether it's over past, present, or future—not for any *reason* but just because you're alive, still have the sense God gave you, and can look before and after. And if you don't have something to cry about in your life, when all that's taken into account, I'll venture to say you don't have much to laugh about either; and you might as well go back to bed and pull the cover over your head.

But anyhow, I think maybe there is something to be said for deciding what you want to have written on your tombstone—that is, of course, if you're going beyond the bare facts of just being born and having died. But then there are a lot of people that don't do much in this world besides that. Like one of my aunts said to me about that bunch of Fosters out at Louisa that just sat there most of their lives waiting for good fortune to drive

THE BURNING BUSH

up to the front door and blow the horn: she said, "O, child, they just slept and et and waited for the weather to change." Of course, it didn't matter *what* weather, you know. And you can look at it one way and say, well, they're just all of them stuff to fill up graves with and let it go at that; but then you get sort of put out with them for being such lilies of the field instead of Marthas in the kitchen because *somebody* has to do the work around here.

But then when you think of some of the things in this world people are quite willing to live and die by—the sort of things they would, I suppose, be glad, even proud to have written on their tombstones, well, it just makes you stop and think, which is the understatement of the day, as far as I'm concerned. Like that fool family of Mercers that we were sort of kin to by marriage or by default or something that they started out perfectly all right except their father married again—after his first wife, who was Mamma's aunt or something, died—and married a Simmons that were all of them the rankest Campbellites you ever saw in your life. And I don't mean the progressive or "organic" kind either: these were the non-instrumentalists (no pianos or organs) in church, and *they* were the only true Church ("*the* Church," they always called it) and "neither shall any man pluck them out of my hand" and so on and so forth till death did you part, Amen. And I used to think, good Lord, if that wasn't something to have put on your tombstone—that that's all you ever had in your life: no real music, no real joy but just debating with Baptists and Methodists and God knows what all, complete with blackboards and tent meetings and tuning forks and everything else, all to prove *you* were mainlining on in to the Almighty but couldn't expect much for anybody else. Well, as that same aunt used to say, that bunch was nothing but just the *first step down,* socially, morally, or what have you. And she *knew* because she used to live over in Johnson County when her husband was alive, where it was all just as thick as two in the bed with Campbellites and Republicans. And after her husband died and she came back

What Do You Want Written On Your Tombstone?

home to live, she said she felt like she had just come out of darkest Africa back into real life.

Well, anyhow, that bunch of Mercers—the Campbellite ones—were all very reasonable on most subjects; and they sure knew how to turn a penny or two and, even more so, hold on to it too. But the one thing on earth they didn't have a particle of sense in the world about was that damned "Church" business. And just to show you, just let me tell you about Cousin Albert Herring that married one of the Mercer women; and he told them in the beginning he was a born and bred Methodist and wasn't planning on making any change, but he would always be glad to have the Campbellite pastors and such like as guests in his home but not to talk to him about religion and that was that. And, when I was growing up, I used to look up to him and think, well, there was *a man among men* and maybe *that's* what they ought to put on his tombstone when he died; and he was just sort of a symbol to me, in lots of ways, like Luther nailing the theses to the church door or Jenny Geddes throwing the prayer stool in St. Giles' Cathedral. But do you know one thing, the last time I was home, my aunt—the one I've been quoting—and I were talking about the Mercers and Cousin Albert, who had just recently died; and I said, "Well, at any rate, that bunch never overpowered *him!*" And she said, "Why, child, they finally got him! I thought you knew."

And then she told me all about his last days, when he got old and feeble and couldn't help himself and then finally really senile; and the Mercers didn't do a thing in this world but haul their Campbellite preacher out from town and put Cousin Albert in a splint-bottom chair—tied in of course so he wouldn't fall out—and have him baptized (they insist on total immersion, naturally) into *the* Church *of* Christ, right there in the Little Hatchie River that ran by their place. And I've never been so disgusted with anything in my life; it almost made me sick, it was so really obscene and indecent—words which I think we've almost forgotten what they really mean now. Well, as far as I'm concerned, what they really mean is treating people like they are things and

THE BURNING BUSH

demeaning and debasing them and yourself and life itself, which you inevitably do in the process. And that last may be your own real and worst punishment for perpetrating such monstrosities. But anyhow, I thought, well, those Mercers have got one more notch on their holster and maybe that's just one more thing for them to have put on their tombstone. And much good might it do them all was what I hoped. Bible study, tuning forks, close communion, and baptism by immersion indeed; they may finally get so exclusive they won't have any room left over for God when they get to Heaven: He won't be enough of a nay-sayer to suit them. So they'll just have to sit there admiring themselves in each other, which of course is what they've been doing all along anyhow.

Well, it doesn't really make much difference who you're talking to or about: everybody has got *something* he'd really like to have written on his tombstone, to sum up his whole life or whatever he feels proudest of having done or having lived by. And sometimes these self-composed epitaphs may strike other folks as a good deal wide of the mark if not downright silly. So I think you'd do well to look over whatever tombstone pronouncement you have in mind and study up on whether it really is what you want to have said about your works and days. Of course, you can't keep other people from writing their own versions of your epitaph, so to speak, which is really too bad because some really dreadful things do get perpetrated that way sometimes.

Like one of the cousins on the other side of the house that married a man from down in the red-dirt country of North Mississippi, which Mamma said there was nothing in world good could possibly come out of—a hardshell Baptist too. And when he died, I want you to know that one of the dear departed's friends or family—but I don't really *want* to know who—sent, as his idea of a "floral tribute," a wreath of bright red carnations, standing on an easel and all that—very elaborate—and, in the middle of the wreath, a baby-blue styrofoam telephone with the receiver off the hook and, printed on the white satin ribbon down beneath, in blue spangles, "Jesus Called." And so they had

What Do You Want Written On Your Tombstone?

AT&T and red, white, and blue to waft the old boy on to Glory with; and I was wondering if there was anything else they had possibly left out when, right there in the middle of the funeral, which Mamma had made me take her to or I'd never have been there in the first place, up rose a woman evangelist named Sister Beulah Scoggins and preached his funeral sermon on the text: "The beauty of Israel is slain upon thy high places: how are the mighty fallen!" And considering that the deceased in-law, who was ugly as homemade sin, had met his end by driving blind-drunk off a bad curve going up one of those North Mississippi hills at eighty miles an hour, I thought they might just as well have left it at "Jesus Called" and said no more about it.

But then some people never learn about the uses of reticence, to say nothing of silence. They're better than charity for covering a multitude of sins, to my way of thinking. On the other hand, all such public noise-making does help to fill up the silence, which is a very terrifying prospect—silence, that is—for half the people you know, anyhow. If it went on long enough, they might even have to sit down and think things over, and then where would they be? They might even have to revise their own tombstone inscriptions, which would really be the same as changing their private estimates of their own lives; and there are not many people you know who are ever prepared to do that, whether on long or short notice. But then, when you come to think of it, there's a very great deal most people are not even prepared to *entertain* in the way of an idea, to say nothing of a thought.

Of course, I suppose you can go too far in the other direction and spend so much time working on what you take to be your epitaph that you don't have time to live—like making a lifework out of who your ancestors were and how much money they had but you don't now: you know, "what Papa said" and "back when things were normal," and that sort of thing. But none of this says anything really about *you*. Not long ago I had a flat tire right at the entrance to a cemetery I was driving by, so I stopped to call my filling station from a telephone booth that was right by the gates (I wondered at the time just who Mother Bell had in mind

THE BURNING BUSH

to use it when they put it there). And I got to wondering what my friendly Texaco dealer would say if I told him to just guess where I was calling from. But then I thought that half the calls I got every day were really made from the cemetery anyhow, whether the callers knew it or not. Maybe they'd been too busy composing their own epitaphs to think about that; and it was really too late for that kind of employment now, though of course they'd be the very last to know it. But then you can't worry about *them* either, any more than you can the ones that never imagine there might possibly be a tombstone in their own lives too. People do go to extremes on subjects like that.

When I was a little boy, my father used to tell me that, if you sang at the dinner table, all your children would be born naked, which always provoked my mother but tickled me. But he also told me that, if you went and stood on a dead man's grave and asked him what he'd died for, he'd say *nothing!* And that used to puzzle me a great deal, especially when Mamma always just said Mrs. So-and-so died because she couldn't get well. And that somehow seemed to settle it. But what Daddy said made you think seriously for a moment, until you saw the joke. But even after that, the serious part lingered on, like an aftertaste in your mouth. What did he die for; what did he live for; what did he want to have written on his tombstone, and was it what could and should have truthfully been written there? Who in the world was ever safe from questions like that? Nobody I knew: that was for sure, self included.

Troubled Sleep

I think our sleeping, like our waking, goes by cycles if not by spells. For weeks on end, we put out the light, close our eyes, and know no more until morning. Then something—I'm not sure what—breaks the pattern; and for days, nights, perhaps weeks, we sleep fitfully, waking frequently in the night, and restlessly, often troubled by dreams which, if not nightmares, are at least troubled ones.

Surely, we need our dreams, whether sleeping or waking; they often tell us more about ourselves than we know in broad daylight. And, in one way or another, we live with them all our lives: they inspire us; they lead us, drive us on, to do whatever it is in the world's work, the business of life, we think we are most fit for. Take away our dreams and we die: that's certain. And even vulgar, tawdry dreams—the kind Jay Gatsby had, for instance—may be better than no dreams at all. Because a dream implies an ideal, a goal, no matter how debased or unworthy it may be. And a hog, even a woodchuck, as in Frost's poem "After Apple-Picking," has no need for dreams. His slumber is that of the animal, not the rational creature; sometimes, it's even hibernation—being dead to the world for a time, a season—something denied us humans.

But what about the other sort of dream—not the ones laid in marble halls and gilded chambers, where each one has always his heart's desire and which, in turn, leave him reinvigorated, on waking, to strive even harder in his quest, his determination to fulfill the bright promise of his particular dream? What about the troubled dreams—old fears, old hatreds which may have festered deep down inside for many a long year, sometimes unknown to us but more often all too familiar, sometimes even shockingly so?

We find, during these troubled dreams, these old unspeakables coming up, like the Prophet's head on the platter out of the

THE BURNING BUSH

cistern; and we may be horrified to have to acknowledge that yes, they've been there all along, though we've not seen them or taken notice of them for years on end. Perhaps that's part of their ultimate terror: we do recognize them so easily and so well. And verily, they're still with us, no matter how far we've come from the times when they were more immediate to our lives and experiences.

Faces, words, deeds we may have thought dead and buried—shameful, shocking, saddening—all of them may suddenly surface, in dreams, like the corpse of some murdered man come up finally from some dark and bloody body of water to seek light and air—and retribution. And we wake in terror, in fear lest they, it, whatever, should be coming to *get* us—that oldest of childhood bugbears, embodied in the oldest of childhood formulas. Sometimes it's our own words and actions which come back to haunt us; sometimes it's those of others. Again, it may be only things we never said or did but stand secretly convicted of by our own consciences, which sleep not even when they may seem to most. And even when we recognize that our grievances, the ones we've never even acted on, may be quite legitimate, that doesn't mitigate their horror as they come screaming, crashing back to us in the terror of literal nightmare. We recognize the animal—our own guilt, whether in the hands, on the lips, or in the heart. And it's still real, after all these years, these many miles. We haven't traveled so far perhaps as we thought.

But it's the more subtle, if less dramatic, troubled sleep that concerns me most now: no witches, no night-fears, no ghosts (and who doesn't believe in them, one way or another?), but vague anxieties, dim disturbances, inarticulate fears, muttering quietly in the twilight troubled state halfway between sleep and waking—talking quietly but clearly, one feels, if necessary, on into eternity. What are they, these troubles which visit us in sleep, not to wake us as in a nightmare but quite literally to trouble, disturb, concern us so that, on waking, we rise somewhat sadder and wiser, if no more fearful?

Perhaps they're signs that we're neither more nor less than hu-

Troubled Sleep

man (Hopkins: "What hours, O what black hours we have spent/ This night! what sights you, heart, saw; ways you went!"). And we do look before and after and pine for what is not, and veiled Melancholy does have her sovereign shrine in the very Temple of Delight. On the other hand, it's not always so easy to dismiss or even deal with those whisperings that come to us in the long watches of the night: have we done all that we could and yet remain even now unprofitable servants; have we loved our neighbors as ourselves; have we forgiven till seventy times seven? Really, truly? And what if there should be no other chance; what if our account is called in now, yea, before the day break and the rising up of the sun? If nothing so dramatic or apocalyptic as this, we may well be concerned with whether we have done our whole duty toward God and man yesterday and the day before, to say nothing of the morrow. And we do lie there taking considerable thought for the morrow: we're not lilies of the field, whatever else we may be; we're convinced of that. So we lie there as the whispers close in round about us, troubling, disturbing, breaking our rest, even burdening us with woes we may feel not altogether ours, certainly not always of our own making.

What do we do? I think finally we thank God, for visions, for dreams, even for nightmares, just as we thank Him for all His Creation, both great and small. And we thank Him for our humanity, which is comprehended in our dreams, both good and bad. Again, Frost in "Tree at My Window":

> *Vague dream-head lifted out of the ground,*
> *And thing next most diffuse to cloud,*
> *Not all your light tongues talking aloud*
> *Could be profound.*

Likewise, in "After Apple-Picking":

> *One can see what will trouble*
> *This sleep of mine, whatever sleep it is.*
> *Were he not gone,*

THE BURNING BUSH

> *The woodchuck could say whether it's like his*
> *Long sleep, as I describe its coming on,*
> *Or just some human sleep.*

The Creation may be but another manifestation of the Creator's Holiness; but He has set man over it, His steward as well as His servant. And it's our stewardship, I think, that gives us the greatest concern: have we multiplied our talents as much as possible; have we been faithful in little things; are we worthy of greater trusts; or must we depart forever accursed into outer darkness as faithless and unprofitable servants?

These are the troubles that differentiate our sleep from the animals', the plants'; we wouldn't be human without them. We ought, I'm sure, to be grateful for what may seem a back-handed sort of gift. Yet we're fallen creatures, and this is hard to do. I know because, for some time here lately, I've been troubled by such sleep, occasionally even by such dreams. What do such manifestations portend, what messages do they bring, if any? God's in His Heaven, but all's certainly not right with the world. Whatever they may mean, they really can't add a great deal to that. I suppose, at last, we take them as we find them—or as they're given to us: significations that nothing really is ever lost, the hairs of our heads are indeed numbered, and no sparrow falls to the ground without particular notice. It—our dreams, our voices, our sleeping, our waking—all somehow hangs together; and it all somehow means, though we see it now mostly through a darkened glass. Finally, we may even come to feel that such knowledge somehow constitutes the ground of a joy which will surely be ours in the fullness of time, even now may give us glimmers of quiet gladness. O, I hope it's so, because that's the way I'm trying to look at it right now. And sometimes it's not easy, I can tell you.

Christmas Sorrows, Christmas Joys

Christmas is strictly for children, I used to think. Of course, I was an only child myself, and I suppose holidays are always better with large families. But we used to have wonderful Christmas dinners—one at each of my uncles' houses. And since there were five brothers (counting my father), it took us the whole two weeks of my school vacation to eat our way through them.

Always there would be a lot of talk about which aunt had outdone the others in what she cooked—but all friendly rivalry, you know. The uncles were merely egging on the ones who hadn't yet entertained the clan, to be sure they would come up to the mark. My mother used to half-brag, half-lament that she was the one who had started the series of dinners, "when she came into the family." But they all welcomed the opportunity to get together and tell over and over again the same old tales that we had all heard a thousand times before, and it used to try my patience something fierce to have to hear them again. As I said, they weren't even new tales—just mostly about when my father and his brothers were growing up out in the country and what all had happened at the schoolhouse (pronounced "schoolouse") and the Methodist church at Maple Grove. I would have given anything to ride off into the sunset on the silver screen with Bette Davis or Clark Gable in a very fast convertible and never hear of Maple Grove again. I couldn't have cared less what "Aunt" had had for Christmas dinner in the terrible winter of 1917, when everybody was dying of the flu so fast they had to hand-make coffins to bury them in, and what one of my uncles that got drafted had had for breakfast when he was stationed up north somewhere during the World War—prunes, I think. But the rest of the family never got tired of it, it seemed.

Of course, I always wanted a *big* Christmas tree—one that would reach the twelve-foot ceiling in our old house. But my parents thought such a tree would be too big and too much trouble

THE BURNING BUSH

and, besides, I had Christmas at all the uncles' houses too—a stocking hung by the chimney at each of them and something to look forward to when I went around with my father to see them on Christmas morning, to find what Santa Claus had brought. I don't suppose anything else in my whole life will ever thrill me the way the sight of my Santa Claus gifts at home used to. Even now I can feel the skipped heart-beat and that thrill-chill at the bottom of my stomach that came when I turned out of the hall into the living room and saw the old silk stocking of my mother's I had hung on a nail on the mantelpiece the night before, all bulging with mysterious shapes, and then a stack of presents piled underneath on the hearth. No joy, no surprise since has ever surpassed it, I think.

But there was something lacking—brothers, sisters or someone to show my presents to, to unwrap them with, and show off to and with. My parents were middle-aged when I was born, and I think they probably found it difficult to enter into the spirit of the thing with me. But there were always the uncles' houses to visit, the cousins (much older than I, of course) to see and to ask what Santa Claus had brought them. And they would smile and bring out their first pair of silk stockings—the girls; and the boys would show me the first rifles of their very own. I thought how wonderful it was to be grown up and wondered whether I would ever live that long.

And how anybody could wait till Christmas Day to open presents I could never understand! One of the cousins, much older than I, was a schoolteacher; so all her pupils gave her presents. But she wouldn't open a single one till Christmas morning. I didn't understand how in the world she controlled herself so well, but I suspected it all had something to do with her being an old maid and not having much other excitement in her life. She certainly wasn't riding off with Robert Taylor into the silver screen or anywhere else.

But those dinners were really unforgettable. Afterward everybody would stagger away from the table and say, "Never again," and "How in the world did we manage to eat so much anyhow?"

Christmas Sorrows, Christmas Joys

One of the brothers, who had really "married out of the family" in every way (his wife was a *Baptist* from the *north* end of the county), even suggested that we all go in together and have just one big dinner, the way his wife's folks did. But my mother just said, yes, she supposed they *would* do that sort of thing and it was not any of it anything to us. And that was the end of that.

My father's oldest brother was an amateur photographer, so every year we had to have a number of "group pictures" made at one or more of the dinners. That procedure involved standing for what seemed like hours in the cold on the front porch while he disappeared under the camera's black hood to see how we all looked. And then one of the uncles would make some remark about how Great-Uncle Albert didn't know he was bowlegged till he came into town to buy a suit of clothes at the age of forty and for the first time saw himself in a full-length mirror at the dry goods store. But his wife, Great-Aunt Tabitha, told him not to be a fool, she had known it for twenty years without saying anything about it. And that would set all the uncles off to giggling, and the pose for the picture would be spoiled.

But sooner or later they would manage to do as an old traveling photographer had instructed somebody in the family years ago when he came through the country taking pictures: "Sit stiddy, look nateral, wink reg'lar, and keep your eyes on the 'feudlam,'" which I always took to be the camera lens. And then the photographing session would be over for another year. But my uncle would always tactfully touch up everybody's gray hair with a lead pencil before he gave the prints around. One year he even branched out and did some tinting of his own; but my mother said there wasn't any point in gilding the lily that much, especially since these lilies might not even be much to begin with.

The dessert at nearly all the dinners was the same: coconut cake and boiled custard. A big thing was made out of passing the little pitcher of whiskey (bourbon, I suppose) around so that everybody could "spike" his custard to his taste. And they all—good Methodists that they were—would giggle and snort as if they were committing all the Seven Deadly Sins in one fell swoop.

THE BURNING BUSH

One time my father even got up and pulled down the window shade, pretending that he didn't want the neighbors to know what we were up to! They all loved this little flirtation with Satan: none of them, of course, ever took a real "drink" in their lives. One year, I remember, my mother even pasted the symbolic Four Roses clipped from an advertisement onto a little brown pitcher she used for the "flavoring," and that brought extra gales of laughter. Of course, there were always one or two holdouts—the old maid schoolteacher who couldn't abide liquor but always had to flavor her boiled custard with vanilla extract, which, as my mother pointed out, was at least 20 percent alcohol. But it didn't do any good; she might as well have saved her breath.

Of course, the family was awfully close—five brothers living there in that one county and not one of them making a move till they had all consulted each other about whatever they proposed to do. And they were all thick with sentiment: I used to be ashamed of the way my father would tune up and cry on what seemed to me very slight provocation—when he told me he'd never known what a man meant by saying he could lay down his life for his children until I was born; or when he told me how much he loved my mother now—more even than when they were married; or how he had gone home to see his mother, whom he adored, during her last illness and had sat for an hour by the fire with his head in her lap. And I suppose my father knew how I felt: instinctively, I would draw back as though fearful of some sort of touch, even an embrace, when he told such things. But he would only smile and say I would understand when I grew older—just one more thing that I would have to postpone until that mysterious time when, it seemed, all of a sudden, blinding knowledge about everything in the world that wasn't in some school book would break over you like an ocean wave. And you would never be the same again.

Sometimes when my uncle was making the annual Christmas pictures, I would look around at all those older people and wonder whether they would all be in next year's picture—as though the frame that caught them might be trying to freeze them in

Christmas Sorrows, Christmas Joys

time, but with dubious results. And I would wonder what changes might take place before another Christmas rolled around. The family conversation at such times might have had something to do with this feeling; practically every tale told concerned at least one person who was dead, and other stories were dated from "the year after Ma died" or "five or six years before Sister got sick with consumption." Death, it always seemed to me, was the uninvited guest at those revels; and his presence hovered behind and above and over every conversation, every remark. Whom would he take next from that picture frame? And every year you could see all the family showing their ages more, both in the pictures and out of them.

I never knew what my parents would have said had I tried to discuss such thoughts with them. I felt they probably would have thought it peculiar or else dismissed it with a laugh; *everybody* died—you took that for granted—but there was no need to *dwell* on it. But I would look at the families of my playmates, and theirs were all much younger than mine. And I knew that, in due course, mine were going to die off earlier than my friends' families. And I would be overcome, at such times, by some sense of coming, inevitable privation: my parents were going to die and die early and I had no brothers or sisters, only much older cousins. It was like knowing, just from an August breeze—or even when there's a cold snap in June—that fall and winter are coming soon and coming inevitably.

It wasn't my parents who were the first to go—to drop out of that picture frame—but the aunt I loved the best because she had no children of her own and seemed to spend much of her life trying to fill up what might have been the emptiness by loving her husband and the rest of the family, and giving of herself over and over to all her friends. And she died right at Christmastime in 1943. Those numerals "1943" to this day still are highly charged for me: when I hear them, I'm automatically reminded of my aunt's death, and date whatever event of that year is being referred to as taking place before or after that.

That was my first real death too—not one you took for granted

THE BURNING BUSH

because the person was really old and it was more or less time for him to die. My aunt was still in her fifties, but she had not been well for many years and finally everything more or less caught up with her. I remember they took down the Christmas tree in my uncle's living room, before they brought her body back home from the undertaker's, then replaced the Christmas wreath on the front door with a funeral wreath. I don't suppose I'll ever forget it till the day I die—death, death at Christmas, when all around one the emphasis was on birth, new life, the Baby Jesus, Emmanuel, God with us, here and now, this day, this time, this season. But for me, it then became the season of death: the Christmas carols mocked my sorrow, with their emphasis on joy, light, peace coming into the world. And I would not be comforted.

Again, I didn't tell my parents. What would they have said? Would they have thought me weak-minded in my grief, or would they just have smiled indulgently and said, well, I was just a little boy (a teen-ager now) and I would understand when I got older. I wasn't going to risk any of that, so I held my Christmas grief closer to me and felt—knew—Christmas would never be the same again. The picture frame had been shattered, there would be an empty place at the table, and after this there would be more. The next year we had no Christmas dinners: my mother wasn't well, and none of the family seemed to feel up to it either. But in another year we began them again and, more or less, went on with business as usual. But I wondered, again all to myself, was anybody really fooled?

The years went by, I grew up, and there were no surprises. The family did start dying off, more places were empty in the picture and at the table. It was all as I had imagined it would be. Yet the family kept on getting together for the Christmas dinners—older and feebler, some of them. And always there would be talk of those who were gone on, those long dead whom I never knew, and death again and always the unseen guest. I really wished we would quit having Christmas dinners. And finally we did, the year after my father died. Only two brothers were left now, but no one felt up to entertaining the whole family at home. And the next generation (my older cousins) really didn't care much about serving a dinner, and really no one wanted to take the trouble. But we had that last dinner at a local restaurant, in one of the private dining rooms. And though no one said anything, I felt that it was somehow indecent for us all to be gathered there, in someone else's house—not even a friend's but one we had rented for the occasion. And again we had a group photograph made; there were not many of us in it now. We couldn't sit long after dinner: the restaurant management obviously wanted to close up and go home, and we understood. But I think we all knew that was the end of the Christmas dinners, though none of us mentioned it.

And it was. A couple of years after that my mother became ill, in what turned out to be her last illness, though it was protracted for many years. I got home only a few times a year from my job in the city; and at Christmas it was mostly a matter of going to see the widows of my uncles, seeing them more and more circumscribed in their activities, leading quieter and quieter lives, unless there were grandchildren to come in and liven things up.

When there were, of course, things were different. Some of the aunts, I decided, were making a business out of the grandchildren thing—a phenomenon I was not unacquainted with in other circles, where it seemed to me (I was not married and thus was disqualified from holding an opinion) most people could be forgiven anything on earth just as long as they had reproduced their kind, which simple fact of biology seemed to cover a multitude of sins and justify all manner of irregularities, personal and public. I even played a game with myself about how some of my friends and family talked of their grandchildren: did they speak of them half-apologetically, or did they speak out loud and bold, or did they merely take it for granted that nothing, nothing in the world, was so important as this living witness of their own continuity and perpetuity? The way some of them even pronounced "children" made the word sound as if it were something holy, sacred, certainly not to be profaned by any skeptical reservations

THE BURNING BUSH

on the part of a childless bachelor. Sometimes it was "*the* children," sometimes "*my* children," or simply "cheeldrun," as though that lingering, loving appellation in itself was a holy talisman against evil, if not alms for oblivion as well.

And of course, all of them and all things gave way to the children at Christmas (had it been that way in my childhood? I didn't remember), for whom no joy must ever be spoiled. Who would ever have introduced death as a guest at any of their holiday tables? Who ever would have had me as a Christmas guest had they known that death stood silently at my elbow throughout? But I had learned early (had seen coming) this guest who would surely sit at all tables sooner or later, whether in the time of Nativity or not. Christmas and its joy only intensified one's sorrow at such times, I had found.

Fittingly, it was my mother's death that seemed to put the final seal on all Christmas deaths for me: she too died a few days before Christmas. Admittedly, she had been out of active life for a long time, and many of her own friends were gone. But hardly any of the family could come to the funeral: they were either too old or else taken up with their own separate Christmas preparations and their children and grandchildren. I wondered, idly in the back of my mind, whether there would be enough on hand to get my mother into the ground. There were, of course, but only a handful, many of them childhood friends of mine. And as we sat there in the funeral home (no one would have thought of having the funeral in church; it would have been more trouble and the sanctuary embarrassingly empty), one of the cousins I hadn't seen in a long time said, "Listen, I know what you must be thinking, but forget about Christmas. I lost my own mother at Christmastime. And I can tell you, it's just something for children and that's that. Of course, I don't have any of my own, but it's not a season for grown folks."

I was inclined to agree with her. Christmas for me, for a good many years, had been a kind of measuring stick against which to judge the present losses and predict the future ones—a milestone rather than a feast. Perhaps, had I myself been different, it would

Christmas Sorrows, Christmas Joys

have been otherwise: but I had no children, no family now, had not really had a family for some time, ever since I left home to go off to school, then to take my first job. I remembered that, as a child, I had always felt closer to God and his Son at Christmas: I didn't know whether I could be crucified along with them (I was diffident somehow about Easter); but I knew I had been born and it was silent and peaceful ("Silent night, holy night"—; "How silently, how silently the wondrous gift is given") yet full of happiness and joy ("Joy to the world, the Lord is come"—; "Yea, Lord, we greet Thee, born this happy morning"—). And I thought, yes, I had been born, could be born again, maybe would be born again if it so pleased God.

That was the old Christmas joy: I remembered it from my childhood. Yet it seemed that my own Christmases now were so crowded with deaths, with ghosts. Was there room for life, for joy? Was I morbid, even selfish—to say nothing of sinful—in my present Christmas thoughts? With my heart so full of Christmas deaths, was there any room for birth? Had I willfully shut out life and joy—a landlord who declared there was no room for them in his inn?

I thought about all this one Sunday afternoon shortly after my mother's funeral, as I attended a service of Christmas music given each year by a big city church. And in the middle of one of the loveliest carols, I suddenly—almost as a surprise—closed my eyes and wept. One by one, my Christmas joys had all been taken from me, the picture frame violated, the places swept from the table; yet surely there was another joy—a joy no man could take away—in what you had been given in such love. Surely, no one who had known such love, such joy, could properly repine. Gone it might well be, but you *had* had it and it had been yours. That had indeed been your blessing, which nothing could ever discredit, compromise. The fact that you had had it was proof that it existed, that other joys might someday be yours too, and it *was* real. Was this the ultimate Christmas joy, the real Christmas gift, made while we were yet sinners, so ignorant, so unworthy? Like all real gifts, it was there whether you chose to

Christmas Sorrows, Christmas Joys

accept it or not; but no one was forcing it on you, which might be the greatest gift of all. I dried my eyes and sat there remembering my Christmas joys and listening to the music until it was time to stand for the singing of the "Hallelujah Chorus" at the end.

PS
3554
.R237
A6
1975

$15.95

PS
3554
.R237
A6

1975